BLONDES, BIKINIS
and
BETRAYAL

EMERALD FINN

FINESSE SOLUTIONS

Cover design by Wicked Good Book Designs
Published by Finesse Solutions Pty Ltd
2022/06
ISBN: 9781925607109

Author's note: This book was written and produced in Australia and uses
British/Australian spelling conventions, such as "colour" instead of
"color", and "-ise" endings instead of "-ize" on words like "realise".

A catalogue record for this book is available from the National Library of
Australia

For Mal. Best husband. Whole world.

CHAPTER 1

"SO HAVE YOU KISSED HIM YET?" MY SWEET OLD AUNTIE ASKED, doing her best to look innocent. Her best wasn't in the least bit convincing.

I almost choked on my avocado on toast. "Aunt Evie!"

I could feel heat rising into my cheeks. Surely I wasn't going to blush? I was twenty-nine years old, for goodness sake. Just because my rather forceful aunt was gazing at me over our brunch with a gleeful light in her eyes, there was no need to react like a twelve-year-old schoolgirl.

Sadly, my cheeks hadn't got the memo. Hastily, I took a gulp of my latte, hiding my flaming face behind the extra-large mug.

"Well?" she prompted, once I finally stopped pretending to drink and put the cup down again. Her giant earrings swung as she tipped her head to one side. Together with the large sunglasses and floppy white hat, they made her look like an old-time movie star. "Curtis is a lovely young man. And I must say, he looks mighty fine in that uniform of his. If I were forty years younger I'd be playing cops and robbers with him myself."

"Aunt Evie!" I protested again, fighting back a smile as I glanced around the diners at the other tables, checking to see if anyone had overheard. We were sitting at the little outdoor café nestled up against the side of the surf club. Over Aunt Evie's diminutive shoulder, I had a glorious view of golden sand and the beautiful blue water of Sunrise Bay. The yellow and red flags fluttered on the beach, marking the area that was safe to swim, and the Nippers ran up and down the sand practising their safety drills under the watchful eyes of the lifeguards. Their shouts and squeals mingled with the harsh squawking cries of the seagulls.

One particularly brave seagull landed close to my feet and strutted around the sandy ground looking for crumbs. Rufus, my golden retriever, eyed the bird from his place under the table, where he was practically glued to Aunt Evie's white-clad knee, before deciding that keeping his gaze firmly fixed on Aunt Evie and her plateful of bacon was a much better idea than chasing seagulls.

"That's better," she said, rewarding Rufus's restraint by slipping him a generous chunk of bacon. He must have swallowed it whole because it disappeared in a nanosecond. "It's good to see you smiling. You've looked so serious all the time lately. You should be having fun. You're only young. Why shouldn't you kiss Curtis Kane or any other man you fancy?"

"I never said I fancied him." There was no point begging her to keep her voice down, since that would only encourage her to say something even more outrageous. She might have been physically small, but everything else about Aunt Evie was big—her personality, her love of bright colours, and, most definitely, her opinions. Luckily for me, everyone at the surrounding tables was busy with their own food, and the wind off the ocean carried the sound of our voices away.

Aunt Evie snorted. "Of course you fancy him. A three-day-old *corpse* would fancy him. He's a good-looking man."

I flinched a little at the mention of corpses. There'd been far too many of those in my recent past. I hurried to steer Aunt Evie back on course. "Well, okay, he is very attractive."

"I'll say! And he has *such* a caring nature."

"Yes, that too." Seeing the way he acted around his six-year-old daughter, Maisie, was the sweetest thing in the world. I had no objection to Curtis Kane—far from it, in fact—but I just wasn't ready to jump straight into a new relationship so soon.

I should have known better than to tell Aunt Evie about my date with Curtis—not that it had really been a *date*, as such. We'd met at this very café for brunch three weeks ago and hadn't seen each other since. We'd texted a few times, but he hadn't seemed like a man desperate to see me again, which, in the circumstances, suited me fine.

"I know what you're thinking," Aunt Evie said, sneaking another piece of bacon to Rufus. As if I couldn't see exactly what she was doing. Rufus gazed at her with an adoration usually reserved for T-bone steaks, and the single-minded focus of a dog who hasn't been fed in at least three decades.

Rufus, it might be added, was an extremely good actor.

"Really?" I sat back in my chair and lifted the heavy fall of my light-brown hair off my sweaty neck. We were into early December now, and the Australian summer was in full swing. It might only be ten o'clock in the morning, but the sun had a definite bite to it. I was grateful for the umbrella that shaded our table. "What am I thinking?"

Aunt Evie's hair was the exact same colour, though she needed the hairdresser's help for that these days. She swallowed a piece of fried egg and stabbed her fork in my direction. "You're thinking that it's too soon, aren't you? Ha! I knew it! Your face is an open book to me, Charlotte Rose."

I rolled my eyes. Normally Aunt Evie called me Charlie like everyone else. She only used my full name when I was in trouble or if she wanted to make some kind of point. Like now.

"It *is* too soon. I only broke up with Will a couple of months ago." And uprooted my entire life as a result. One glimpse of my fiancé in bed with my best friend had been enough to drive me right out of my corporate life in Sydney, to a whole new world here in Sunrise Bay. Or Sunny Bay, as it was affectionately known among the locals.

"Oh, pish tush. What a lot of rot. You're well rid of Will. You shouldn't waste another minute of your life thinking about him or regretting him or letting him hold you back in *any* way."

"We were meant to be getting married on January the fifteenth. I was supposed to be having my last fitting for my wedding dress on *Monday*. I really think it's a little early to be leaping into another man's arms. Don't you? I mean, seriously?"

Aunt Evie put down her knife and fork and gave me a wry look from under her outsized sunhat. "Seriously? You're asking the wrong person, darling girl. I don't even buy green bananas anymore, as poor old Peggy used to say. I'm not as young as I used to be and I'm not about to waste any of the time I have left. Seize the day, I say. Carpe diem."

"You're not exactly at death's door," I protested. *Green bananas.* Honestly! Rufus wasn't the only one at this table with a flair for the dramatic.

The twinkle faded from her blue eyes, so like my own, as she reached across the table and captured one of my hands between her two wrinkled ones. Aunt Evie was a very well-preserved seventy-two, and to look at her perfectly made-up face you would think she was a good decade younger, but her hands showed her age. I loved those hands. They had all but raised me after Mum died.

"Will hurt you, I know, and it's perfectly understandable to take some time to grieve. But it's been two months. He's not worth the dirt on your shoes and if you let him continue to spoil your life, you're giving him power over you. Move on. Live a little. Not all men are like that. The good ones are much more reliable."

I squeezed her hand, her soft skin warm against mine. "He's not spoiling my life anymore, I promise you. I just want to take things slowly this time." And I wasn't even a hundred per cent sure that Curtis was interested in me as anything more than a friend.

"There's a time for slowly and a time to go after what you want." Aunt Evie's tone left me in no doubt which one she thought this was. "I might never even have met your uncle if I'd taken things slowly. I saw him on the other side of the hall and I liked what I saw, so I marched right over there and asked him to dance in front of all his friends."

I grinned. I'd heard this story many times, but it always made me smile. Uncle Andy had been the opposite of Aunt Evie in almost every way—quiet where she was loud, tall where she was short ... and absolutely besotted with her. I could picture tiny, sophisticated Aunt Evie so clearly, marching in and taking the lanky young farmer's world by storm.

"Uncle Andy never stood a chance."

She patted my hand, smiling. "Relationships are like riding a horse, I always say. As soon as you get thrown, you should get straight back up and get on again, before you lose your nerve entirely."

A *highly* inappropriate image of riding the delectable Curtis Kane popped into my mind at her words, and I hurriedly changed the subject before I started blushing again.

"Did I tell you about my photo shoot with the twins?"

"Heidi's boys?"

Our friend Heidi had adorable five-year-old twins. I'd already had one very successful, if a little boisterous, photo shoot with them. It had helped launch my fledgling photography business.

"No, these twins are older. Samantha Middleton and Jessica Garcia. Do you know them?"

Aunt Evie knew enormous numbers of people in Sunny Bay—and had opinions on most of them, too—but she shook her head. "No, can't say as I do."

"They just turned thirty and they wanted a photo shoot to commemorate the big occasion."

Aunt Evie snorted into her coffee, clearly considering thirty to be no big deal. From my own point of view at twenty-nine, it certainly felt momentous. I'd always imagined I would be married by the time I was thirty, maybe even with a baby. Still, there was no point thinking about that now. I'd come to realise that I'd had a lucky escape when my wedding to Will fell through, and I was determined not to dwell on might-have-beens.

I pulled one of the small, printed canvases out of the carry bag I had with me to show Aunt Evie. "This is them."

The photo showed two identical grinning blondes, arms around each other. They both wore pink T-shirts with *She's the pretty twin* printed on them, with an arrow underneath pointing to the other person. Their hair was cut in short bobs that framed their happy faces and they both wore a pink baseball cap with the word *Princess* on it spelled out in diamantes. Jess had told me that they had bought those caps on a trip to America when they were in their early twenties, and had treasured them ever since.

"But this is the last time we are *ever* wearing identical outfits," Sam had said, only half joking. To me, she added,

"Our mum used to dress us in the same clothes until we got to high school. It was *dire*."

"Just for the photos," Jess had promised. "It'll be fun!"

"They're pretty girls," Aunt Evie said.

I nodded. "This one's Sam." I pointed to the woman on the right, whose tanned arms were more toned than her sister's. Sam liked to work out and it showed.

"It's a lovely photo. They should be very pleased."

"I hope so." I smiled proudly down at the grinning sisters. Taking photos of happy people was turning out to be far more rewarding than working in the HR department of a big accounting firm in Sydney. Who would have guessed? I felt a thrill of pride in my work that I'd never experienced before and every day brought a new challenge. I still got excited every time a new client contacted me.

I checked my watch. "I'll have to head off soon. I'm meeting them at Sam's house to deliver these."

"Did you drive? Why did you bring Rufus?"

"No, we walked along the beach. Didn't we, boy?" Rufus's silky ears pricked up and his tail thumped briefly against the ground. "Sam's house is only around the corner from here. It didn't seem worth bringing the car when it's such a lovely day for a walk."

Aunt Evie frowned at me. "Are you sure you're not just avoiding driving?"

"No, it truly is just around the corner, in Fitzgibbon Street." I *had* been a little nervous about getting back behind the wheel after my car accident, but I was over that now.

Aunt Evie pushed her empty plate away and patted her lips delicately with the paper napkin. Amazingly, her lipstick was still in place. I'd have to find out what brand it was. Mine never stayed on that long, if I even bothered to wear any. "Oh, speaking of driving—did you hear that someone in town won the big lottery this week?"

I blinked. It wasn't always easy to follow the direction of Aunt Evie's thoughts. "What's that got to do with driving?"

"There's a sign up in the window of the newsagent. I saw it when I was stopped at the lights on the way here. It says they sold the winning ticket."

"In the jackpot lottery?"

She flapped her hand vaguely. "I don't know. I don't follow that kind of thing. Something with balls?"

"You mean the lotto?" I guessed. "Or the Powerball?" That got drawn on Thursday nights.

Her face brightened. "Yes, that's the one. It was worth seven million dollars, apparently."

"How exciting! Imagine having seven million to play with. I wonder who won." I drained the last of my coffee and started to dig through my wallet for money to pay the bill. There was considerably less than seven million dollars inside.

"Don't worry about that, darling, I'll pay. You paid last time."

"I can't go sponging off my retired aunt," I protested.

"Nonsense," Aunt Evie said in a tone that brooked no disagreement. "I am a Woman of Means, whereas you are a Struggling Artist."

I had to laugh at the way she phrased it. I could almost hear the capital letters. I gathered my bags and bent to drop a quick kiss on her perfumed cheek. "Thank you. As long as I don't have to starve to death in a garret for my art."

She smiled at me. "As if I would let you starve."

CHAPTER 2

SAM'S HOUSE WAS A NEAT BRICK BUNGALOW WITH A BRIGHT RED front door. A large jacaranda tree, still blooming, took up most of the front yard. It was an older-style house, with no garage, only a carport on the side. There was no car parked there.

The one jarring note in the neat picture was the letter-box, which had been uprooted like a tree blown over by a gale. It lay on the grass by the path to the door, the ball of concrete that had once anchored it in position now torn out of the ground, leaving an unsightly hole. The letterbox itself was dented and its lid no longer shut properly. Maybe the postie had hit it with his motorbike? If so, he must have been roaring along the footpath like a speed demon.

I knocked on the gleaming front door, but no one came. I checked my watch. Just after midday. I was five minutes late.

"I wonder if she's forgotten?" I asked Rufus, who ignored me in favour of sniffing for lizards among the sun-drenched rocks that edged the small garden by the porch. Red geraniums grew there, almost the same colour as the door.

I knocked again, louder, but in the absence of a car, I had little hope that Sam was home. Hopefully she'd been out somewhere and was running late too.

"She's not home." Sam's neighbour was watering her own garden. She was a tired-looking woman in her forties with limp grey hair and a general air of dissatisfaction with the world. She eyed me morosely over the low fence separating the two properties.

"Do you know where she is?" I asked.

The woman shrugged, spraying water over her hydrangeas. "Haven't seen her since she left for work yesterday. You're wasting your time."

"Oh. Well, I'll give her ten minutes. She's expecting me."

"Suit yourself."

I sat down on the front steps to wait and the woman turned her back, clearly not interested in chatting. Rufus gave up his hunt and collapsed at my feet—or rather, *on* my feet, which seemed as though it should have been uncomfortable, but he settled himself with a sigh of contentment and closed his eyes. I stroked his soft head and he licked my hand without even opening his eyes.

A grey sedan turned into the street. It slowed as it approached, then stopped completely across Sam's driveway. The driver leaned across and lowered the passenger-side window.

"Are you okay? Can I help you?" She was a blond woman about my age, wearing a navy blue blazer over a cream silk blouse, as if she'd just come from the office. Not Sam, unfortunately.

"I don't know," I said. "Do you know where Sam is?"

"No, sorry. I can ring her, if you like."

"That's okay, I already tried that. She's not answering. Are you a friend of hers?"

"Yeah. I just live over there." She gestured with one hand, indicating a house a bit farther along on the other side of the street. "The cream brick place with the green roof. I guess Sam is having a more fun weekend than I am. I'm just on my way home from a conference in the Hunter."

"The Hunter doesn't sound so bad." It was a famous wine-growing region about an hour from Sunrise Bay, full of boutique wineries and world-class restaurants.

She grinned. "The Hunter's beautiful, but the conference was putting me to sleep. I was meant to stay all afternoon, but I snuck out early. I've been talking taxes since Thursday night—that's enough taxes for anyone. Hopefully Sam shows up soon. She often runs late to things, you know."

"Does she? Well, I won't give up hope just yet, then."

She gave me a wave, then closed the window and continued down the street. I watched as she parked in the driveway of the cream house, took a small suitcase out of the boot of her car, and went inside.

A few minutes later, a pink VW pulled into Sam's driveway and a blond woman got out and gave me a cheerful wave.

I stood up. "Sam?"

She grinned. "No, Jess. Isn't Sam here?" She glanced at the empty carport, then eyed the fallen letterbox with surprise.

"Nope."

Jess rolled her eyes as she shut her car door. "I sent a text to remind her, but she didn't reply. I hope she hasn't forgotten."

"Do you want to wait for her or shall I just give you these?" I indicated the bag that held the two canvases.

She came towards me with quick steps, car keys clenched in her hand. Something dangling from her keyring caught the sun and flashed light into my eyes.

"Let's wait—if you don't mind? I want us to be together when we see them." She bounded up the steps to the front door and dug around among the keys on her keyring. The dangling charm caught the light again and I saw it was a large letter S covered in diamantes. These women really had a thing for diamantes. "Come in—I'm sure Sam won't mind if we wait inside. It's hot out here, isn't it?"

"Sure is." I nodded at her keys as she swung the door open. "I thought you'd have a J on your keyring. Does your husband's name start with S?"

She laughed. "No, his name's Leo. This is S for Sam. She has a matching one with a J for Jess. It's a twin thing."

"Must be nice to have a sister who's so close," I said as I followed her into the cool of the house. "Not you, Rufus! Stay outside. Stay! I won't be long."

He gave me a mournful look as I shut the door in his face.

"It is," Jess said, leading the way into a neat lounge room. It had polished wooden floorboards, cream leather lounges and the biggest TV I'd ever seen hanging on one wall. "You've always got a built-in ally—or someone to fight with, I guess." She laughed. "There were some battles when we were growing up, as you can imagine. Two girls sharing a bedroom and everything else. But we're tight now. I know she'll always have my back."

I thought a shadow crossed her face as she said that last bit, but she turned away and moved farther into the house, calling for her sister, so I couldn't be sure.

I looked around the room, as neat and attractive as the garden had been. A massive arrangement of roses sat on the dining table at the far end of the room. It gave me flashbacks to the unwelcome bouquets my ex-fiancé had showered on me recently, and I looked away hurriedly. There was a long buffet in the same honey-coloured wood as the table in the dining room, with half a dozen photos grouped at one end. The largest was of the twins, in that long-legged teenage stage, wearing bikinis and outsized sunglasses. They were balanced on the arms of an enormous anchor which had been placed upright in front of a lighthouse, laughing at the camera.

In a moment Jess was back, shaking her head. "Well, I

don't know where she's got to. Have a seat." She indicated one of the cream lounges and I sat. The long glass coffee table in front of me had a pile of magazines neatly stacked at one end and a bunch of birthday cards scattered across its surface.

Jess tried calling her twin again, but it went to voice-mail and she hung up and sent a quick text instead. "Sorry about this."

A Powerball ticket peeked out from inside one of the birthday cards. I nodded at it. "Maybe she's the big winner and she's gone on an epic shopping spree."

Jess glanced at the card and pulled a face.

"Something wrong?"

"No, it's nothing. It's just that Lauren always gives her a Powerball ticket for her birthday. Uses the same numbers every year."

"Who's Lauren?"

"One of Sam's friends."

"Not one of yours?"

"Lauren and I ... don't get along." She picked up the card and read the message inside, then threw it back on the coffee table. The ticket fell to the floor, but she didn't pick it up. I hoped Sam didn't mind her sister reading her mail. Still, being twins, they'd probably done a lot worse to each other over the years. "Ever since high school, she's been trying to get Sam to herself. Her birthday's a week before ours, and she and Sam always make such a fuss over each other's birthday, as if it's not mine, too. They give each other lottery tickets and flowers and go out to lunch. I think Lauren wishes *she* was Sam's twin instead of me. She's never wished me happy birthday in my life." She lifted one shoulder in what was probably meant as an uncaring shrug, but I could see she felt resentful.

"That's rude. Happy birthday, by the way."

"Thanks. Leo and I went out to dinner at the Metropole. It was lovely. Nice to get some alone time for a change."

The Metropole was a grand, if slightly faded, hotel on the southern headland overlooking the beach. I loved its art deco interior and its air of quiet elegance. Not that I'd ever stayed there—but Priya and I had been there for drinks after work a few times. Priya was one of my new book club friends, and she was always trying to turn book club meetings into alcoholic celebrations.

"Is alone time hard to come by?"

She sighed. "A little. We're living with Leo's mum and dad and his two younger brothers at the moment. It's a pretty full house."

I gave her a sympathetic smile. "Saving up for a deposit?"

"We had a deposit. We were building our own house, actually. But the builder turned out to be a crook and declared himself bankrupt. Took our money and we're still stuck in Luis and Gabriela's spare bedroom."

"Oh, that's rough." I bet I knew exactly which builder she was talking about. The same thing had happened to my book club friend Sarah.

Silence fell and Jess started fidgeting with her keys. I

tried to look at my watch without being too obvious about it.

"Are you sure you don't want to see the photo?" I asked. I mean, she'd seen it on the website. Both sisters had checked out the photos from the shoot and chosen the one they wanted printed on canvas. But seeing the finished product in real life was different. The camera shop I used did a good job with the printing—the photos came out rich and vibrant and looking like a work of art.

"No, I'll never hear the end of it if I peek without her," she said. "And I'm in enough trouble already."

"Oh?" I didn't mean to pry, but they'd seemed perfectly comfortable with each other at the shoot. If they'd had a fight since, I was happy to be a listening ear if Jess wanted to talk about it. I liked her. Sam, too. They were smart, professional women who were quick to laugh and seemed to really have their lives together. Once I had my business off the ground, I was hoping to emulate them.

"Well, we had a bit of a disagreement a few weeks ago." She glanced at me quickly then looked down at her keys again. "Nothing major, just one of those tiffs that sisters have, you know."

I didn't know, since I didn't have a sister, only a brother on the other side of the world who wasn't much of a communicator, but I could imagine. I nodded encouragingly.

"Well, the photos were my way of saying sorry." She sighed. "I really thought she was over it, but I guess she still hasn't quite forgiven me if she's not here. Though it's not like her to stand *you* up."

"Do you think she's all right?" I didn't want to alarm her, but if the grouchy neighbour was right ... "Her neighbour told me earlier that she hasn't been home since she left for work yesterday."

Again that shadow crossed Jess's face. "That's pretty standard for Sam. Free as a bird, she is. If she meets some guy at the pub, well, you know how it is when you're single and you don't have any responsibilities. And she's been talking about a new guy from the gym lately. She often doesn't get home until the morning after."

Well, more power to Sam, then. I was single and that party lifestyle wasn't for me, but if she liked it, why not? She was a good-looking woman, so finding guys to party with wouldn't be a problem for her.

I checked my watch again. It was almost twelve-thirty and I had other things to do today. If Sam was still sleeping off last night's excesses, who knew when she might turn up?

I stood up. "In that case, I might come back later, if that's all right with you."

Jess jumped up, too. "Of course. We've wasted enough of your time already. Look, I'll give you a ring once I hear from her and we can organise a new time to get together." She cast a rather wistful glance at the bag containing the two canvases. "I'm really sorry about this."

"Don't worry about it. I had brunch at the Surf Club café with my aunt this morning. It was only a couple of minutes out of my way."

I opened the front door and Rufus greeted me as if I'd returned from the dead, leaping up to lick the highest possible point he could reach. Then we said goodbye and he set off for home, tail held at a jaunty angle, checking over his shoulder once in a while as if to say, "Hurry up, then! I've got things to do."

CHAPTER 3

I LIVED IN A SMALL TWO-BEDROOM DUPLEX WITH DISTANT glimpses of the ocean—if you cared to hang over the balcony rail, or stand on the toilet to peek out the bathroom window. It was only a short walk to the beach, so I didn't mind the lack of a water view. On still nights, I could hear the waves shush-shushing on the sand, which soothed me to sleep better than any lullaby.

My next-door neighbour, Mrs Johnson, had moved out only last week. She'd been wanting to move to the same retirement village that Aunt Evie lived in for some time, but had felt as though she couldn't, because she had her late husband's dog to consider. Sunrise Lodge didn't allow pets, so she was stuck, which was a shame since she didn't even particularly like dogs, but she felt she owed it to her husband to look after his beloved pet. Then I moved in next door and Rufus, starved of attention, more or less adopted me. She gave him to me with her hearty blessings, and promptly moved out.

When Rufus and I turned into our street, we found a removalist's van parked in Mrs Johnson's driveway.

"Looks like we've got new neighbours, boy."

Rufus glanced up at me, mouth open in a doggy grin, then turned his attention back to more important things, like identifying who had weed on the telegraph pole lately. He lifted his leg and left his own calling card for the neighbourhood dogs, then trotted happily after me.

A silver station wagon was parked in the street outside the other duplex, its hatch open. As I drew level with it, a man not much older than me came out of the house and strode towards the car. He was tall and thin, with curly dark hair and a neat beard, and he was wearing a Star Trek T-shirt that had seen better days. There was a hole in the shoulder and the hem was hanging down. Either it was much loved or he'd quite sensibly decided not to risk his good clothes on moving day. Maybe both.

"Hello," I said, stopping by the car. He smiled at me as he hefted a big box of books out of the car. "I'm Charlie. I'm your next-door neighbour."

He juggled the box onto one hip and stuck out a hand. "Nice to meet you. I'm Jack. Jack Watson."

I shook his hand, which was a little dusty. "Welcome to the neighbourhood. I'm pretty new myself. Or have you been living in the area already?"

"No, just moved here from Brisbane." He had green eyes that stood out dramatically in his tanned face, and they lit up when he smiled. "Decided I needed a new adventure and got myself a job at the hospital here."

"You're a doctor?"

"A nurse, actually."

I glanced into his box, which was filled with old-looking books with cracked spines and battered covers. I spotted a familiar title.

"Oh, I'm reading *Middlemarch* at the moment, for my book club! Do you like it?"

He looked sheepish. "Oh, no! Now I have to admit that I haven't read it. These ones belonged to my grandma. I'm more of a science fiction guy, myself." He laughed. "I promised Grandma I'd read all of them one day, but that was twelve years ago and I've been carting this box around from house to house ever since."

He had such an open, friendly smile, I bet all his patients loved him. He'd be a sunny presence in a hospital room.

"Maybe you should join our book club."

"Maybe I should." Then he noticed Rufus sniffing around his car and his smile dimmed. "Is that your dog?"

"Yes. His name's Rufus." I hoped he wasn't a dog-hater. Unwelcome memories of Will resurfaced, and I pushed them away.

"He doesn't chase cats, does he?" There was an anxious light in his eyes. "I love dogs myself, but Sherlock has other ideas."

"Who's Sherlock?"

"My cat. He's nine. He's never been fond of dogs, but now that he's a grumpy old man he doesn't cope well with them at all—and he's not that fast on his feet anymore, either."

"Wait. Your name is Watson and you named your cat Sherlock?"

He laughed. "That's one classic that I *have* read."

"Where's Sherlock now?" I asked.

"I shut him in the spare bedroom while I get all my stuff moved in."

Jack's duplex was a mirror image of mine—two bedrooms upstairs with a bathroom in between, and downstairs a combined living and dining room plus kitchen and laundry. Not palatial by any means, but big enough for one person.

"I'll have to keep him inside for the next couple of weeks until he gets used to the new place," he added with a smile. "Not that he wanders far. He's way too lazy for that. He's really more of an indoor cat."

Rufus ambled over to us and sniffed Jack's knee, then licked it thoughtfully, leaving a damp mark on his jeans.

"I've never seen him chase a cat before." To be fair, I hadn't known him that long either, but we'd ranged all over town together and he'd never paid any attention to cats or even really bothered with any dogs we'd passed beyond a quick sniff or a vague wag of his tail. He always seemed far too focused on his explorations. "I think Sherlock will be fine."

Jack hefted the book box into his arms again. It must have been getting pretty heavy by now. "That's good. Well, I'd better get on with this. I've got a lot of unpacking to do and my first shift at the hospital tomorrow."

"You have my sympathies. It's not that long since I moved in myself." It had taken me a few weeks to get settled and unpack all the boxes. "Good luck. You'll sleep well tonight."

"I'm sure I will. See you later." He headed inside, manoeuvring past the removalists, who were lugging a massive TV inside.

My phone rang not long after I went inside myself. It was Priya, my book club friend and news hound extraordinaire.

"Hi, Priya. What's up?"

"Don't even ask," she said. "My mother is driving me crazy."

"Why? What's she done?" I put the phone on loud-speaker and left it on the kitchen bench so I could make myself a sandwich. I'd had a big breakfast but it was almost two o'clock and I was getting hungry again.

"She's trying to marry me off again," Priya said in tones of deep disgust. I could picture her dark eyes flashing. Priya, like Aunt Evie, wasn't one to hide her feelings about anything.

I paused with the fridge half open and looked back at my phone in surprise. "Marry you off *again*? Why, does she do this often?"

"Every year at about this time." Priya sighed. "It's my birthday in January and the approach of Christmas seems to remind her every year that I'm still single. It's like clock-work. Once the shops start playing Christmas carols, she starts playing matchmaker."

I knew Priya's parents' marriage was an arranged one, but that had been while they were still in India, and it was a long time ago. They'd moved to Australia before Priya was born.

I slathered peanut butter over a slice of bread, ignoring Rufus's pleading looks. He loved peanut butter. "She's not serious though, is she? I mean, she can't force you to marry anyone, can she?"

"Why do you think I moved out? No, she can't force me, she just starts with the guilt trips until I agree to go out with whoever the latest candidate is."

"That doesn't sound so bad." I cut off a tiny portion of my sandwich and threw it to Rufus, who snatched it out of the air with delight.

"No, but that's just the beginning. Then she starts leaving bridal magazines around and telling me how much she longs for grandchildren. Last Christmas she even gave me a book of baby names for a present, just in case I hadn't got the hint."

I laughed. I'd met Priya's mum recently—she was my new doctor, in fact—and she'd seemed down-to-earth and ruthlessly efficient. I had trouble picturing her as a master manipulator. "Are you sure she wasn't joking?"

"Well, of course she *said* she was, but I know the truth. And she's relentless. Last year, she managed to squeeze in *two* 'suitable boys' before Christmas. One was a doctor and the other was a lawyer. Prime husband material in Mum's eyes."

"It could be worse," I said cautiously. "All you've got to do is go out with some guy to keep your mother happy."

Priya groaned. "I'll be thirty-two in January and she's getting desperate. This year she's insisting on a family dinner with the guy and his parents. I just know that she and the other mother will spend the whole night planning our future. By the end of dessert they will have named all the grandchildren and decided which school to send them to. I don't think I can take it."

I swallowed a big bite of peanut butter sandwich before I answered. "So just say no. Tell her you're busy that night or something."

"*No* is not really a word that my mother understands. Anyway, enough of that. That's not why I rang you. I was wondering if you had a copy of *Middlemarch*. Heidi has already borrowed the library's only copy and I thought if you were finished I could read yours before the meeting."

"You're kidding, right? Have you seen how big this book is? I'm still only a quarter of the way through." By the time I finished wading through it, a busy reporter like Priya would have no chance of getting it read in time. "Maybe you should see if you can get an audiobook."

"Is it any good?" she asked.

"It is, actually." The classics weren't really my cup of tea—I preferred books with dragons and lots of magic, whereas the book club wouldn't read anything that wasn't written by someone who'd been dead for a long time, preferably a century or two, at least. *Middlemarch* was managing to hold my interest, despite a distinct lack of dragons. "There are a lot of unhappy marriages in it. Maybe you should get your mum to read it—it might put her off the idea of marrying you off, if she could see the mess that some of these people are making of it."

Priya snorted. "You don't know my mother. Nothing

can put her off when she's got her mind set on something. But it sounds a bit dire. Maybe I won't read it, especially if it's that long. Who has the time for fictional characters' unhappy marriages? Life is too short when you've got a determined Indian mother and a potential marriage of your own to avoid."

"Honestly, it's a good book. I'm sure you'd like it."

She sighed. "Don't mind me. I'm just grumpy. It's been a bad week."

"Why? What else has gone wrong?"

She sighed again, a big, gusty sound of disappointment. "I just can't believe it. *Finally* something happens in this sleepy little town and I can't even get the story."

"What do you mean?"

"The Powerball winner. I could have got my name into every newspaper in the country if I could only write a feature article on the winner. But of course the winner would have to choose *not for publication*. Just my luck—an anonymous millionaire. I'm good, but even I can't make a personal interest story out of that."

"Don't give up hope. The way people around here gossip, their identity will probably come out before long."

She grunted. "I should get you to ferret them out for me. You've turned out to be such a super sleuth."

"Only unintentionally," I said, shuddering at the memory of the murders I'd been caught up in. "No more sleuthing for me! Nothing but the quiet life from here on."

I really should have known better.

CHAPTER 4

ON MONDAY MORNING I DROVE INTO TOWN TO GRAB SOME groceries from the little supermarket there. One of the perks of working for yourself was that you could sneak time for personal errands into the workday—especially if your business was only just starting out, and there wasn't all that much to be done. As I walked past the newsagent, I saw the sign in the window that Aunt Evie had mentioned, done in hand lettering on a sheet of white cardboard.

WE SOLD THE WINNING TICKET!! it proclaimed in excited block letters. ONE LUCKY SUNNY BAY RESIDENT IS $7 MILLION RICHER!!!

Seven million was a lot of money. I stared at the sign for a moment, lost in a pleasant daydream of what I would do with that kind of money. I'd buy a big house on the beach. I'd take my friends away for a week on a fabulous tropical island. Maybe a month. Heavens, if I had seven million dollars I could probably afford a whole year. That kind of money didn't even feel real. It was too big a sum.

I'd travel all over the world and visit all the places I'd longed to see. Rome and Venice. London. Paris. Disneyland. Hawaii. I could take Aunt Evie. Or even ...

A certain handsome policeman's face flashed into my mind and I abruptly dismissed the daydream. I had *not* won seven million dollars, and I was wasting time standing here on the footpath.

Inside, I bought some birthday cards and a gardening magazine. Maybe now that I had a little duplex instead of an apartment I could get a garden going. As I paid the lady at the cash register, I asked if she knew who had won the big prize.

She shook her head. "If I had a dollar for everyone who's asked me that since Friday morning, I'd have almost seven million dollars myself. The lotteries office didn't tell us. All I know is that it was an unregistered ticket that was sold from our shop."

"How exciting!" I said. "Imagine being that person."

"Every man and his dog has been imagining it. I can't tell you how many tickets I've sold in next week's Powerball since the news got around." She snorted. "As if we'd sell the winning ticket two weeks in a row! It would be like lightning striking twice in the same spot. Rarer, even. People are crazy, but I'm not complaining."

People just wanted the dream—a little hope that their lives could be magically improved, too. The cost of a ticket was a small price to pay for a week's worth of daydreams.

"Perhaps they're hoping some of the winner's luck will rub off on them."

"Do you want a ticket?"

"No, thanks." That was the other reason I would never win a life-changing amount of money—I never bought lottery tickets.

Over at the IGA, I stocked up on dog food for Rufus and lots of fresh fruit and veg for myself. The mango season was in full swing and I grabbed a whole tray of the sweet-smelling treats. I had one up to my nose, inhaling its delicious scent, when I saw Jess Garcia approaching.

"Hello!" I started transferring my goods onto the conveyor belt at the checkout and she got into line behind me. "You're not working today?"

"No. I only work Tuesday to Thursday, so I have a nice four-day weekend every week."

"Lucky you! What do you do?"

"I work for a conveyancer," she said.

We chatted the whole time the checkout girl was scanning and bagging my groceries. Jess's phone rang as I was paying and she turned slightly away to take the call. I wasn't paying any attention until I noticed a sudden stiffening in her posture and an urgency in her tone that set my spidey senses tingling.

"Everything okay?" I asked when she hung up.

She turned to me, her face strained. "That was my friend Delia. She's a policewoman."

"I know Delia." I'd run into her a few times lately in her professional capacity. "Is everything okay?"

"She said they've just found Sam's car."

I put a hand to my throat. "Sam's had an accident?"

"No." Her face had lost all colour. "The car's been burnt out and dumped. Delia wanted to know if I'd seen Sam lately. They've been trying to contact her." She put her basket down on the conveyor belt and looked at me uncertainly. "I have to go to her house right now. What if she's—? I have to go." But she made no move to leave. She chewed her lip for a moment. "Are you ... would you come with me? I'm scared to go alone."

"Of course. Did you drive?"

She shook her head. "I just dropped in to pick up a few things on my walk."

"My car's outside. I'll drive you."

I led her outside and dumped my groceries in the boot. She got into the passenger seat and put on her seatbelt, moving like an automaton. But when I started the engine she whipped out her phone, as if the sound had jolted her back to life, and called someone on speakerphone. I heard it ring once, then go straight to voicemail: "Hi, this is Sam ..."

She ended that call and started another. "Blakely and Associates," said the voice on the other end. "Beverley speaking."

"Hi," Jess said. "Can I speak to Sam?"

"Sam's not here today."

Even I felt nervous, hearing that. Jess started to shake.

"Henry, then."

"Putting you through."

In a moment, a man's voice came on the line. "Henry Blakely, can I help you?"

"Henry, it's Jess. Sam's sister. I'm trying to get hold of her. Have you seen her?"

"Not since Thursday. Does she still have that migraine?"

"What migraine?"

"She texted me on Friday morning to say she wouldn't be in to work because she had a migraine."

Jess dropped the phone in her lap and hugged herself with shaking hands. "She didn't come into work on Friday?"

Sam's neighbour had told me she'd seen Sam leave early Friday morning. If she hadn't been going to work, where had she been going? And if she had a migraine, why was she going anywhere?

Maybe she'd been on her way to the doctor. Or the chemist, to pick up some medication. But then she'd never come home. I chewed my lip, my stomach twisting into uneasy knots.

"No," Henry said. "Is everything all right? Is she sick?"

"I don't know," Jess said, so quietly it was a wonder Henry could hear her at all. As we turned into Sam's street, she hit the button to terminate the call.

I pulled up outside and threw open my door, but Jess sat, still clutching her arms around herself.

"Are you coming?" I asked.

"Sam never had a migraine in her life," she said, staring at me with wide, frightened eyes.

I got out of the car and went around to open her door. "Come on," I said. "There's probably some perfectly simple explanation for all this. Maybe Sam reported her car stolen and the police lost the report."

"But where is she? And why isn't she answering her phone?"

"I don't know." I held my hand out to her. "Let's go and find out."

She took my hand—hers was cold and clammy—and let me help her out of the car. I stayed close as we marched up the path to the front door. Despite my encouraging words, I had a very bad feeling about this. The house looked just the same as it had on Saturday morning with its cheerful red front door and matching geraniums blooming in the garden by the steps. The broken letterbox still lay on the grass, looking out of place against the neatness of the rest of the garden.

Jess's hands shook so much she couldn't get the key into the lock, and after three tries I gently took the bunch of keys with its sparkly S attached and opened the door myself. A wave of smell so bad I almost gagged hit us as we stepped inside. It smelled as though the contents of Sam's freezer had been left to go bad in the sun.

"What is that *stench*?" Jess whispered, and then she was off, running down the hall, following the atrocious smell.

I ran after her, trying to breathe through my mouth. The smell got worse the further into the house we got. She stopped in the bedroom doorway and I crowded up behind her, afraid of what I might see.

Flies buzzed in the room, battering against the window and swirling around the dangling light fitting.

But there was nothing horrifying in sight, and for a moment I felt a vast relief. Then Jess dropped to her knees and twitched up the valance that covered the darkness under the bed.

Jess screamed, high and anguished. I saw an arm, puffy and discoloured, the fingers like waxy sausages. Behind it, the shadowy shape of a body curled on its side. Bile rose in my throat as I grabbed Jess's shoulder, stopping her as she reached under the bed.

"Don't touch her. This is a crime scene."

"Sam! Sam!" Jess wailed.

She collapsed against my legs, nearly knocking me down. I steadied us both and tugged on her arm. "Get up. Get up, Jess. Come with me."

The next few minutes were a nightmare. She didn't want to leave her sister, but her body had lost all its strength. She wasn't a big woman, but I almost had to deadlift her off the floor. Then I half-carried her back down the hallway, her sobs tearing at my heart.

I meant to take her outside, out of the terrible smell, but I lost the struggle as we staggered back into the lounge room at the front of the house. She slid sideways and would have fallen to the floor except I manoeuvred us so that she collapsed onto one of the pale leather lounges instead. She curled up into a ball of misery and cried.

Once I had her settled, I pulled out my phone and dialled emergency.

"What service do you require?" the voice on the other end asked.

"Police," I said. "There's been a murder."

CHAPTER 5

To THEIR CREDIT, THE FIRST POLICE WERE ON THE SCENE IN
under five minutes, but it was the longest five minutes of
my life. I felt so useless, just sitting on the lounge next to
Jess, awkwardly stroking her arm.

While we waited, I tried to remember what we had
touched. The front door, the valance and part of the
bedroom floor today—but what about Saturday? Had Sam
already been dead, stuffed under her own bed, while we'd
been sitting in her peaceful lounge room? What an awful
thought.

We'd both sat on these lounges. Had I touched the
coffee table? I couldn't remember for sure, but I didn't
think so. Jess had picked up the birthday card from Lauren
and the Powerball ticket had fallen out. It still lay on the
floor where it had landed, slightly under the glass coffee
table. Poor Sam. The ticket certainly hadn't brought her
the good luck her friend had been hoping for.

The pile of birthday cards made me tear up. So many

people, wishing Sam the best for her birthday, probably with "many happy returns". But there would be no more birthdays for Sam. She would never turn any older than thirty.

I blinked, looking around the room. In all the photos Sam was smiling the big, warm smile I'd seen in our own photo shoot. She was tanned and fit, glowing with health and happiness. There were a lot of photos of her alone, all glammed up for a special occasion. Some were with a man, though it was a different one in every photo. The only one of her with her twin was the one I'd noticed last time, on the sideboard in the dining room.

"Would you like a glass of water?" I asked, getting up. I needed to do something. Anything.

I was halfway to the kitchen before Jess replied. "No."

That was probably for the best. The whole house would most likely be part of the crime scene, and I shouldn't really be touching anything. I paused in front of the photo of the twins and frowned. The other girl wasn't Jess after all, though from across the room her blond hair had been enough to fool me. But I now saw she looked quite different, rounder in the face, with a bigger nose and sharper chin. Her hair was up in a bun. The white stone of the lighthouse behind them made a nice contrast to their tanned brown bodies and bright, colourful bikinis. They had their arms around each other, grinning at the camera, two girls enjoying their summer.

Someone knocked on the door, then pushed it open and walked straight in. It was Delia Backhouse, her police hat pulled down firmly over her short, dark brown hair.

She was about my height, but she looked tiny compared to the man who followed her in. Curtis Kane was well over six feet and built like a professional footballer, his dark hair cropped short in a military-style cut.

Delia went straight to the lounge and sat down next to Jess, drawing her into her arms. Jess turned into her friend's shoulder and broke out into a renewed bout of weeping. Curtis looked at me, his jaw set in a firm line, concern in his rich brown eyes.

"Are you all right?" he asked in a low voice, and I felt a strong urge to throw myself into his arms and sob on that broad chest.

"I'm okay." I wasn't usually the type to sob on anyone's chest, broad or otherwise. It was perfectly normal to feel a little overwhelmed after making such a grisly discovery. If I felt relief at seeing him, it was only because I could now hand over responsibility for the whole horrible business to the experts.

He indicated with a jerk of his head that he and I should go outside, so I followed him onto the front porch and he pulled the door closed behind us.

"Delia will calm her down," he said quietly. "Homicide is on the way. They'll want to talk to her—to both of you. Are you sure you're okay? You look very pale."

I nodded, though I'd started to shiver. It was better out in the fresh air, without that terrible smell to remind me of the horror of the bedroom. I just needed a moment to pull myself together.

"I have my jacket in the car if you need it," he said. "You're shaking."

I tried a smile, though it came out a little wobbly. "You can't be always lending me your jacket. I might forget to return it again and then how would you win the Best-dressed Policeman Award?"

An answering smile softened his stern expression. "I can't win it every year; it makes the other officers jealous. Besides, it would give me an excuse to visit you again."

I looked down at my feet. He hadn't seemed to be in any hurry to visit me.

"You're always welcome," I said. Did that seem overeager? "Maisie, too."

"Why don't you sit here in the sun?" His arm came around me and he guided me to the steps. He helped me sit down, as if he thought I'd fall over if left to my own devices.

"Thanks."

"Where's the body?" he asked.

"In the main bedroom. Under the bed."

If he was surprised by that answer he gave no sign. "Wait here."

He went back inside and was gone for a few moments. When he came back out I was sitting with my eyes closed, face turned up to the sun.

He sat down beside me with a sigh. "Okay. Tell me everything that happened since you got here."

I did. He made notes in a notebook, though mostly he just listened. He was a good listener, not interrupting except to ask for clarification now and then. It occurred to me that being a good listener was probably an excellent trait for a police officer.

"And why were you here?"

"I happened to be with Jess when Delia called her to tell her about Sam's car. She asked me to come with her to the house. I think she realised even then that something terrible had happened."

He was quiet, gazing out unseeing at the street. He was so close I could feel the warmth of his body and smell the clean, fresh scent of his aftershave.

He put his notebook away. "It's good to see you again. I spent a week in Sydney on a training course, and I've been pulling double shifts since I got back. Work's been crazy."

Was he trying to apologise for the lack of contact? I sneaked a sidelong glance at his strong profile and tried to think of something to say that showed I was an independent woman who most certainly hadn't counted the number of texts he'd sent since our date (five) or how many days it had been since he'd last texted (seven).

An unmarked car pulled up behind Curtis and Delia's cruiser and two men got out. I recognised Detective McGovern's unruly grey hair and sour expression. He and I had clashed before. A look of annoyance crossed his face as he saw me sitting with Curtis, but his face was a professional mask by the time he and his partner reached us.

"Kane." He nodded at Curtis. "I'll get you to set up a perimeter. Miss Carter, how are you?"

I stood up so he wouldn't be looming over me. That put me higher than him, since I was on the step and he was still on the path. I could tell it annoyed him, which gave me a warm, if childish, glow of satisfaction. "I've been better."

"Did you find the body?"

"Jess did, but I was with her."

"And who is Jess?"

"Jessica Garcia. She's the victim's sister," Curtis said. He stepped aside to allow the two detectives to climb the steps onto the porch. "She's inside with Delia."

"In the crime scene?" His frown showed what he thought of lax policemen who allowed witnesses to trample over crime scenes.

"The body is in the bedroom. Delia and Jess are in the lounge room."

"The whole house is the crime scene," he said frostily. "You know better than that."

"Jessica is distraught," Curtis said. "And since she had already been in the house, I didn't think there was any harm in letting her stay."

Detective McGovern said nothing as he pushed past Curtis and went inside. His partner followed him with a muttered, "Excuse us."

Inside I could hear him talking to Delia and Jess.

"I hope you're not in trouble," I said to Curtis.

He shrugged, clearly unconcerned. "There's no such thing as a pristine crime scene. Witnesses, people who've been there previously, even the weather can mess things up. The crime scene guys will sort it all out. I'm not going to drag that poor woman out into the street when she's just discovered her sister's body."

A white van pulled up and more people piled out, men

with serious faces lugging equipment, and went inside. Sam's neighbour had come out to water her garden, though I was sure that was only a pretext so that she could watch the goings-on next door, since she never shifted from the same spot near the fence. Those hydrangeas were going to drown.

Detective McGovern returned and took Jess and me into the backyard, where he sat us down separately, Jess at the small outdoor table by the back door, and me over by the fishpond in the back corner of the yard. It occurred to me then that perhaps Curtis had had another reason for taking me outside as soon as he'd arrived. The police wanted to make sure that Jess and I didn't coordinate our stories.

That made me feel odd. "Am I under suspicion?" I asked Detective McGovern when he strode across the grass to join me.

I could hear more people moving around inside the house now, their voices drifting through the open back door. I heard the click of a camera shutter too. The police photographer had arrived with the other crime scene investigators. I hoped they took Sam's body away soon. It seemed horrible to leave her there, stuffed under the bed like an old pair of slippers.

"The investigation is at a very early stage," he said, which didn't answer the question at all. Then he asked me all the same things that Curtis had already asked me, to which I gave him the same replies.

His partner interviewed Jess at the same time. I couldn't hear what they were saying, but she seemed calmer now. She dabbed at her eyes as she spoke, but she was no longer sobbing uncontrollably.

Detective McGovern said he would take a longer statement from me at the station later, at which time I would be fingerprinted, so that they could eliminate my fingerprints from the ones they found at the scene. He scowled at me as he said it, as if he thought I'd wilfully run around and contaminated his crime scene.

When he was finished with me, he said I was free to go. Delia came out of the house at the same time to offer to drive Jess home. Jess accepted gratefully and Delia walked us through the side gate to the front yard. I was thankful we didn't have to go through the house again.

The blond woman who'd stopped her car on Saturday to ask me if I was okay was walking a sweet little spaniel towards us. She rushed over when she saw Jess.

"What's going on?" she cried. "What's happened?"

Now that I saw her more clearly, her face tugged at my memory. In a moment, I had it—she was the woman from the photo at the lighthouse, older now, but still recognisable. The one I'd mistaken for Jess at first.

In real life they weren't that similar. Only their height and hair colour was the same. She was a slimmer build than either of the twins, and her hair was pulled back in a long ponytail.

Jess's lower lip trembled. "Oh, Lauren. Sam's dead," she said baldly and started to cry again.

So this was Sam's best friend. The poor woman's hands flew to her mouth and she stared at Jess in disbelief. "No. No no no." She glanced wildly from Jess to Delia and me. "She can't be. I only saw her the other day. I was talking to her on Thursday night."

"I'm afraid it's true," Delia said.

I admired her calm. She was Jess's friend—she must have known Sam, too. This couldn't be easy for her.

"Oh, Jess!" Lauren threw her arms around Jess's neck and burst into tears.

I had to look away, tears pricking my own eyes. I wished there was something I could do to ease their pain, but there wasn't. I crouched down to pat Lauren's dog. He was a King Charles Cavalier spaniel, mainly white, with brown ears and a few brown splotches on his back. He leaned appreciatively against my leg as I stroked his soft, curly ears.

"Jess, let me take you home," Delia said after a few moments. "Can I call someone for you? Leo, maybe, or Gabriela?"

"I'm sorry," Lauren said, releasing Jess and wiping at the tears that still streamed down her own face. "Me crying all over you isn't helping. I'm so sorry."

Jess nodded, still unable to speak, and Delia put her arm around her again. "When you feel up to it, we'll have to get your fingerprints. Yours too," she said to me.

I nodded. "Detective McGovern told me. So they can eliminate ours from the ones they find ..." I almost said, "at the scene" but that felt too harsh and clinical, so I just added, "I'll come down to the station this afternoon."

Lauren sniffed back tears. "You'll need mine, too, then. Mine must be all over that house. We were in and out of each other's places all the time. That's my house over there." She pointed at the cream brick house five or six houses down.

Gently, Delia nudged Jess down the path towards the street and the waiting police car.

"Why would anyone kill her?" Jess stopped at the broken letterbox and turned tear-filled eyes to Delia. "She never hurt anyone. Who did this to her?"

"We'll find out," Delia promised. She had an open, friendly face, but now there was a steely glint in her eyes that promised she would leave no stone unturned in the search for this killer. She eyed the letterbox. "Do you know anything about this?"

"That was Kai," Lauren said.

"Who's Kai?"

"A guy at the gym. He was her new personal trainer. They got a little bit more personal than just training, too."

Delia frowned. "Why would he destroy her letterbox?"

"He has a short fuse. I was texting her from my hotel room on Thursday night because I was bored, and she said they'd had another fight."

"What about?" Delia asked.

"She didn't want to talk about it." Her hand flew to her mouth and her eyes widened. "Oh. Do you think *he* could have killed her?"

CHAPTER 6

When I let Rufus out on Tuesday morning there was a strange thumping sound coming from next door. Yawning, I wandered across to peer over the fence. A guy in shorts and a high-vis shirt had his back to me, using some large contraption to drive holes into the grass outside Jack's back door. The holes weren't very big, probably only a handspan across, and at first I could make no sense of what he was doing.

When he moved on to the next hole he noticed me watching him.

"Oh, hi, Charlie." It was Nick, Andrea's date to Molly's wedding. Andrea was the local librarian and another of my book club friends. I'd been so busy checking out the holes that I hadn't realised it was him.

"Hi, Nick. What are you doing?"

"Putting in a deck for the new owner."

"Owner? I thought he was renting." Surely Mrs

Johnson hadn't managed to sell her house so quickly? I hadn't even seen a For Sale sign go up.

"No, he's definitely buying it, otherwise he wouldn't be putting in the deck. But I think he might be paying her rent until settlement—he needed to move in before the sale was finalised so he could start work at the hospital." He pushed his sandy blond hair aside and wiped sweat from his tanned forehead. Despite the early hour, it was hot already. "I'll be happy when I finish digging the holes for the posts. This is hard going."

"Looks like a big deck." I had a large, paved area outside my back door, but our block was sloping and Jack's back door was higher off the ground than mine. Currently four plain concrete steps led down to the grass from his back door. The deck would be a nice addition, giving him some more entertaining space. Since his duplex was the mirror image of mine, I knew it was pretty small inside. Plenty big enough for one person, though. "How long will it take you?"

"Not long. Three or four days." He put the hole-digger down and took a drink from his water bottle. "Did you hear about the murder?"

"Yeah." I didn't mention that I'd been there when the body was found. Then I'd be stuck recounting gory details and it was too beautiful a morning to be thinking about that.

"That poor woman." He wiped his mouth and put the lid back on the bottle. "I used to see her down at the gym all the time. Never spoke to her but she certainly seemed popular. Such a shame."

He and Andrea were both members of the same gym in Waterloo Bay. That was how they had become friends. I hadn't realised it was the same one that Sam used, though I should have known it was likely. Waterloo Bay was a bigger town than Sunrise Bay, but that didn't mean it was *big*. There weren't many gyms in the local area. "Did you ever see her with her personal trainer?"

"Yeah, all the time. Why? Do they think he killed her?"

I shifted uneasily. I didn't like starting rumours but I was curious to see what he knew. Besides, word would get out fast enough when the police started asking questions. And they *would* be asking questions, after what Lauren had said about him. "I heard that they were going out. I just wondered what he was like."

Nick raised his eyebrows. "Going out? It wouldn't surprise me, though it could cost him his job."

"Really? Why?"

Nick shrugged one shoulder carelessly. "The gym has a no-fraternising policy. I think they're pretty strict about it, too. Professional relationships only between clients and staff."

"That seems a little unusual."

"They had some trouble a few years back with a trainer who was hitting on all the female clients so they brought it in. Once bitten, twice shy, I guess."

"But you think they might have been going out?"

"I'm not saying they were. But once, I was about to go into the change room and Sam came out."

"Out of the *men's* change room?"

"Yes. I asked if she'd gotten lost but she just laughed.

And then, Kai came out a minute later, looking pretty pleased with himself, although that changed when he saw me. Seemed a funny place for a client consultation. From the look on Sam's face, I'd say they were getting pretty hot and heavy in there. That kind of thing could lose him his job if management ever found out about it."

But surely that was no reason to kill someone? I mean, it would suck to lose your job, but you could get another one. And, sure, there weren't too many gyms around here, but there must be a ton in Newcastle, which was only an hour's drive away. No one would kill another person just to save themselves a commute, would they? That had to be the worst motive for murder I'd ever heard.

"Seems a bit risky. You'd think they'd control themselves until they were somewhere more private. Or at least *he* would. It's *his* job."

If you were going to lose your job for kissing someone at work, it would be a lot easier to just *not* kiss them. Then you could save yourself the bother of murdering them afterwards. I shook my head. It was ridiculous. There had to be more to it than that.

"Yeah, you'd think. But maybe that added to the thrill." He shrugged. "And then other times they were barely talking to each other. They seemed to blow hot and cold. I reckon Sam was the type to enjoy keeping a fella guessing."

"And Kai? What type is he?"

Another shrug. "I don't know him that well. He's polite enough, but he doesn't volunteer any personal information. One of those quiet Asian types. A little surly, maybe."

"Oh?"

"On the short side, softly spoken, but there's something about him ... I wouldn't want to get on his bad side, you know? He's freakishly strong." He sighed enviously. "You should see his shoulders. Anyway, where did you hear they were dating?"

"Oh, around." I'd be here all day if I told him the whole story. "I was chatting to one of Sam's friends recently." And Lauren had seemed pretty certain about it.

I tried to imagine myself getting so caught up in a new relationship that I would randomly kiss a guy in public places even though it might cost him his job—and failed. Although my imagination did manage to produce some rather nice images of kissing a certain policeman, so it wasn't a total waste of time.

Don't get sidetracked, Charlie.

"But I got the impression it was a pretty new relationship," I said.

"It would have to be. The guy only started working at the gym a few weeks back."

Rufus wandered over and shoved his wet nose into my hand. I glanced down and he gazed up at me expectantly. Someone was ready for breakfast.

"And if they were so wrapped up in each other that they were sneaking into the change rooms together it doesn't seem likely that he would kill her," I said.

Nick scratched thoughtfully at his neck. "Maybe not,

but, like I said, he's *strong*. He could easily manage it. Do you know how she died?"

"No." That was the truth and I was pretty happy about that. All I'd seen was a hand and a dark mass behind it, and that was enough.

"It's just that I saw him lose his temper once and it wasn't pretty. Punched a wall hard enough to put a hole through it." He shook his head, examining his own hands as if trying to imagine how that would feel. "I wouldn't be surprised if he was on steroids. That can make a person pretty unpredictable. Moody, you know? Liable to fly off the handle over nothing." He looked down and said in surprise, "Speaking of holes, did you know you had a massive one under your fence?"

I laughed. "Yes. That's Rufus's hole."

Right on cue, Rufus stuck his nose under the fence and Nick crouched down.

"Oh, hi there, fella." He patted Rufus's head. Rufus accepted this as his due but didn't bother squeezing all the way through. He was clearly too focused on getting his breakfast. Instead he pulled his head back out after a moment to give me another meaningful look.

"Okay, okay. You're so impatient. You'll get your breakfast in a minute."

Punched a wall. Kicked the letterbox, or whatever Kai had done—it seemed as though he had no issue with letting his feelings out. Maybe that was what attracted Sam to him. Perhaps she liked the excitement, the unpredictability.

For myself, I preferred someone a little more dependable. Again, Curtis's handsome face came to mind, with very little effort on my part. When had he become the standard that I held all men to? I hardly knew the guy, when all was said and done. I'd thoroughly enjoyed the breakfast we'd shared—even though somehow my appetite, usually hearty, had deserted me with his gorgeous brown eyes and dazzling smile on the opposite side of the table. But the lack of communication since then suggested he wasn't as interested as ... As what? As I was?

Ridiculous. I had just come out of a five-year relationship with a lying, cheating snake and I wasn't ready to commit to anyone else yet, no matter how beautiful their eyes or dazzling their smile. A girl needed a moment or two to get her breath back. Just because I felt a little thrill of excitement every time I saw him didn't mean anything. I was twenty-nine, not nineteen.

"He's a lovely dog," Nick said, abruptly bringing me back to the present moment.

Said lovely dog had just wiped a slightly muddy face on my jeans and was now gazing at me impatiently. Again.

"He is." I brushed ineffectually at the mud but only succeeded in spreading it further. "His name is Rufus."

"How old is he?"

"I don't know, actually." Mrs Johnson had given me his bowl, his bed, his lead, and lots of information about him, but I hadn't thought to ask that question.

"He's a rescue, is he?" Nick frowned over the fence at the canine in question. "You don't often see a purebred in a shelter. And he looks like a pedigree retriever."

"He is." His pedigree papers had been among the many

things that Mrs Johnson had handed over. I should check them; they would have his date of birth on them. "But I haven't had him very long. He used to live next door but his owner wanted to move into a retirement village, so she gave him to me."

"I love dogs," he said. "Got two of them at home. Never could stand cats. It's always been dogs for me."

"Well, some people are like that," I said, stroking Rufus's silky head. "They're either cat people or dog people."

He nodded. "Andrea's a cat person. She's got three. Have you noticed she's always got cat fur on her clothes?"

I hadn't, but maybe I wasn't watching Andrea as carefully as he was. I tipped my head to one side, considering him. Did he fancy her? I'd thought he might, when I saw them together at the wedding, but Andrea had laughed it off, insisting they were just friends.

"It's Andrea's birthday next week," I said casually, testing the waters.

"Really?" His eyes lit up. "I should get her something, don't you think? We're gym buddies, you know," he added quickly. Maybe too quickly.

"Yeah, she told me." *Gym buddies.* I looked down at Rufus to hide my smile. Sure, Nick, gym buddies bought each other birthday presents all the time.

"I might get her some flowers. Women all like flowers, right?"

While that was probably true, if you really wanted to impress Andrea, there were better ways to do it. I gave the would-be Romeo a little nudge in the right direction.

"You should get her a book." I could almost guarantee there would be nothing a librarian would like more.

"But she's got so many," he said. "And I'm not much of a reader myself. I wouldn't know where to start."

"A new Ephram Jobbs came out last week," I said, naming a writer I knew from our book club discussions that she liked. "I don't think she's got it yet."

"Great idea," he said. "Thanks, Charlie." He rubbed at the back of his neck. "Well, it's been nice chatting, but I'd better get back to work. These holes aren't going to dig themselves."

"See you later."

Rufus ran to the back door and looked back at me expectantly as soon as I began to move. *Finally*, his expression said. *A dog could starve to death around here waiting for breakfast.*

I opened the door to let him in. "Has anyone ever told you that you are a drama queen?"

CHAPTER 7

I worked on my website for most of the day, uploading photographs I'd taken and generally tinkering with the layout. I had a booking for another wedding just before Christmas—a friend of Molly's had seen her wedding photos and promptly decided that Uncle Herbert probably wasn't going to be a good enough photographer after all, and rung to see if I was free. I also had a portrait session for a local author booked and a couple of family photo sessions. Christmas was getting closer and people were starting to think about presents for Grandma, and a nice family portrait was always a good option.

So I wasn't exactly swamped with work, but I had expected that it would take time to build up my business and for word to get around. I was pretty happy, considering I'd only been going a few weeks. Charlie Carter Photography was off to a good start.

About four o'clock in the afternoon, Rufus, who had been lying on my feet or thereabouts most of the day, yawned hugely and rolled onto his back. His tongue lolled out of his mouth and his jowls flopped to one side.

"You look very relaxed there," I said, grinning down at my beautiful stupid dog. *My dog.* How long had I waited to have my very own dog? And to think, if I'd married Will, I'd *never* have been able to have one. He thumped his tail lazily at the sound of my voice and I rubbed his soft belly, not sure who enjoyed it more. I pushed my chair back. "Come on. You'll get fat and lazy lying around here all day. Let's go for a walk."

At the magic W word he scrambled to his feet, ears pricked, tail wagging madly. He almost knocked me down in his rush to get to the front door.

On the beach, a brisk breeze took the sting out of the sun's heat. Sunset wouldn't be until nearly eight o'clock, but the light had lost its dazzling midday brightness, and the long shadows of the sand dunes stretched almost to where the waves broke on the shore.

Rufus trotted along, his plumed tail lifted jauntily into the air, stopping occasionally at some clump of seaweed or bit of driftwood that had been washed up by the sea. He largely ignored the seagulls who gathered in watchful flocks on the sand, and they returned the favour. If they'd been cockatoos it might have been a different story—he seemed to have a personal vendetta against the large sulphur-crested ones that were so common in the area. Perhaps it was the terrible noise they made that he objected to.

He ranged a long way ahead, but frequently returned to me as if to make sure I was still okay, giving me a quick wag or sniffing at my hand to check in. If he was impatient with my slow progress he gave no sign. He was just a dog out for a walk, living his best life.

For myself, I was enjoying the feel of wet sand between my toes and the occasional rush of a small wave over my feet. The wind tugged at my hair, but I had tied it back in a firm ponytail, since eating my own hair wasn't one of my favourite things and it was frequently windy down on the beach.

There were plenty of other people on the beach too, although it wasn't crowded, but I didn't see anyone I recognised until I was almost at the flags that marked the safe swimming zone in front of the surf club. Then a small voice squealed, "Charlie!" and Maisie abandoned the sandcastle she had been building in favour of throwing her sandy damp self against me and squeezing her small arms around my waist.

"Hi there!" I returned the cuddle, even though her bright pink swimming costume was rapidly leaving a large wet patch on the front of my shorts. "What are you doing? Are you building a sandcastle?"

She released her death grip on me and grinned up at me, her wild curls loose around her cherubic face. Her stick-thin arms and legs were tanned a deep brown, showing that an after-school trip to the beach was probably a regular occurrence. One of the benefits of living in a town like Sunrise Bay. Her dark brown eyes, the same shade as her father's, were alight with enthusiasm. I looked around to see if I could spot my favourite policeman but sadly, he was nowhere in sight.

"Yes. Come and see." She tugged me over to her creation which was a sandcastle so covered in seaweed it was difficult to see what shape it was underneath. It stood right at the edge of the damp sand, well above the current water line. She had dug a small moat around the seaweed lump with her bright pink spade and had clearly been ferrying buckets of water up the beach to fill it. I could have told her that was a losing game, as the water soaked into the sand and disappeared faster than she could ship it in, but she didn't seem fazed by her disappearing moat.

A woman was stretched out on a towel nearby, though far enough away that I wasn't entirely sure she was with Maisie until Maisie spoke to her.

"Look, Mummy! This is my friend Charlie."

So this was the famous Kelly. She wore a white one-piece swimsuit that had clearly never been anywhere near the water. It looked impossibly glamorous against her golden tanned skin. Her blond hair was up in a fashionably messy bun and large sunglasses covered half her face. She glanced at me with a lack of interest that couldn't have been more obvious if she'd had a flashing sign above her head that said, *don't talk to me.*

"Hi," she said, unsmiling.

"Hi," I said. "Nice to meet you."

Which was a blatant lie, but politeness had been ingrained in me from an early age. *Thanks, Aunt Evie.*

Various people had told me about Kelly, but no one had mentioned how astonishingly beautiful she was. Of course, I knew she was a model, which meant she couldn't exactly look like the back of a bus, but I wasn't prepared for the glamorous reality. Even sitting on a towel watching her kid playing in the sand, she looked as though she could have been on the cover of *Vogue*. And they wouldn't even have needed any Photoshopping. She was model-thin, of course—maybe a bit too thin, but she had cheekbones so sharp they could have cut glass, and a full, pouty mouth. Her legs seemed to go on forever. She was lying down, but I could tell she was tall, much taller than me. That hair probably reached down to her waist when it was freed from its bun. She reminded me of a young Elle MacPherson and made me briefly annoyed with the universe that allotted such incredible beauty to a lucky few while leaving the vast majority of us looking far more ordinary.

And someone, I could tell already, who absolutely did *not* deserve that allotment.

Maisie, bless her, didn't notice the coolness of her mother's greeting, and went on excitedly chattering. "Charlie's a photographer, Mummy. I bet she could take really nice pictures of you."

"I bet," Kelly said, again without a flicker of expression, which somehow managed to convey a great deal anyway—like utter disdain laced with incredulity.

"I'm sure your mum knows a million photographers already," I said.

"But I bet none of them are as good as you," Maisie said loyally.

Was that an eyebrow twitch? It was hard to tell behind the outsized sunglasses. I was starting to wonder if Kelly had overdone the Botox. Maybe she was just naturally expressionless.

Or rude. That was definitely an option.

"Have you got your camera with you?" Maisie asked. "You could take some photos of my sandcastle."

"Just my phone," I said. "Not my big camera. Maybe another time I can bring it with me to the beach and take some nice photos of you. You could build another sandcastle."

Maisie clapped her hands. "Then I'd be a model like you, wouldn't I, Mummy?"

Kelly lowered her sunglasses so that she could frown at her daughter over the rims. "Sweetie, real models don't work for free. Is Charlie going to pay you for your time?"

Maisie's face fell at the obvious disapproval in her mother's tone. But she persevered. "But Charlie's my friend, Mummy. She doesn't have to pay me. *I* don't mind." Clearly the idea of starring in her own photo shoot appealed to Miss Maisie.

"Charlie is a professional with a business to run. I'm sure she knows how these things work." Kelly cast a cool glance my way. "If she's going to make money out of putting your image on her little website, she should pay you for it."

I was sorry I had suggested it now. The disappointment on Maisie's face tugged at my heart and I had only meant to take some photos to give to Maisie herself. I hadn't been trying to profit from her.

Although I *had* actually been thinking of asking Curtis if I could take some shots of his photogenic daughter for my website. Just of her chubby six-year-old hands holding seashells or the back of her curly head looking out at the ocean. But knowing I had thought about that now made me feel dirty, as if I'd been planning to exploit the child, when that had been the furthest thing from my mind. She was just so darn cute, with her round freckled cheeks and wild, sun-streaked curls. She hadn't got that from her mother, whose long locks wouldn't have dared to be untamed.

Those big pleading brown eyes didn't hurt, either. I didn't know what to say, but fortunately Rufus saved me from having to answer her mother's cool attack by bounding up and shaking water all over us.

Maisie shrieked happily and patted his big, goofy head. Kelly flinched away as if she were about to be mauled by a savage beast, though she was out of range of the shaking. If possible, her expression turned even colder at the arrival of this obvious menace to life and liberty.

The menace licked Maisie's face, which was currently right at lick level, since she was kneeling next to her sandcastle. She giggled happily.

"Isn't he cute, Mummy? His name's Rufus." And then the inevitable question: "Can *we* have a dog?"

"You know Mummy's allergic to animals," Kelly snapped and Maisie's mouth turned down in an unhappy line.

Wow. I should introduce Kelly to Will. They'd get along famously.

"You can ask your daddy to bring you over to play with

Rufus any time," I said unthinkingly. All I wanted was to cheer her up, but Kelly turned her icy gaze on me.

"I heard you'd been seeing my husband," she said.

I blinked. Her *husband*? She made it sound as though I was some kind of homewrecker, when from all I'd heard she'd done a pretty good job of wrecking that home all by herself.

"We've met," I said, just as coolly. It would be no business of hers if I *was* seeing Curtis, but I didn't think one date—that wasn't even really a date—counted as *seeing* someone.

That eyebrow of hers rose infinitesimally again. "You've *met*," she repeated flatly. "Maisie told me you'd had breakfast together. I assumed you knew each other ... quite well."

Was she implying ...?

She *was*. I glanced at Maisie, the little traitor, who was busy trying to feed seaweed to Rufus, unaware of the insinuations that were going on over her head. To be fair, it wasn't her fault if her mother jumped to conclusions that were quite unfounded.

"Breakfast at a *café*," I said, feeling a blush warm my cheeks, though it was just as much anger as embarrassment. "I met him there in the morning. Though I'm surprised you care who your *ex*-husband has breakfast with." I made sure to emphasise the "ex".

Or who he slept with, for that matter. They'd separated when Maisie was three. Curtis was well and truly free to live his own life now. He could be sleeping with a whole parade of women if he wanted to and it still wouldn't be any of her business.

"I can't have him bringing just *anybody* into my daughter's life," she said. "Maisie's at a very impressionable age right now."

Like I was such a bad influence? What did she think I was—an axe murderer? Or just some floozy who was going to lead her innocent daughter astray? Get her hooked on photography, maybe? Oh, the *danger*.

I gave her a smile that was as big as it was fake. "Well, let's hope his taste in women has improved in the last few years."

And then I called Rufus to heel and strode off, leaving her open-mouthed and fuming in my wake.

CHAPTER 8

THE BEACH WAS USUALLY MY HAPPY PLACE, BUT AFTER MEETING the so-delightful Kelly, I stalked past the surf club and up onto the street. I needed a change of scene.

How dare she look down her annoyingly perfect nose at me? *Maisie's at an impressionable age.* The hide of her! Had she considered not doing drugs in front of her impressionable daughter?

Guilt tinged my angry thoughts at that. Okay, so I had no proof she was actually doing drugs at all, much less in front of her daughter. I sighed, following Rufus's floofy tail down the street towards the shops. I was only bad-mouthing her in the privacy of my own mind—I could say what I liked. Or so you'd think. But my annoying sense of fairness wouldn't let me accuse her of doing something so awful without proof.

Sometimes being a good person was so *limiting*.

Rufus was ranging far ahead, so I stepped up the pace. I could walk off my bad mood and get some exercise at the same time. I powerwalked after him, trying to think soothing thoughts and admire people's front gardens, but my anger simmered away persistently.

How dare she assume I was sleeping with Curtis just because we'd had breakfast together? I stewed on that for a while. Maybe *she* was the type to jump into bed with a new guy so fast, but that didn't mean *I* was.

But hang on—why was I so mad? My daydreams lately had been full of getting Curtis horizontal—and there was absolutely nothing wrong with that. We were two consenting adults. We could have sex fifty times a day if we wanted to.

I grinned as I followed Rufus past the bakery. Well, maybe not *fifty*. That might be expecting a little much from any man.

My mood improved by my own silliness, I considered the question more calmly. Why *did* I care that she had accused me of sleeping with him?

And then I had my answer. It wasn't about the sex at all. It was because she'd implied that I wasn't *worthy* of sleeping with Curtis. She didn't know me from a bar of soap, but she'd judged me already and found me wanting.

Which was so patently unfair, she'd offended my sense of justice. It was almost enough to make me leap into bed with Curtis just to spite her. That was another thing about me—I held grudges like a champion.

"It's not as though *she's* a shining example of anything," I muttered. Except maybe how to destroy a marriage in one easy step. Again, something she had in common with Will and my erstwhile best friend, Amy.

They should all get together and run a masterclass or something. They could call it How to Blow Up Your Life in One Simple Lesson. They could have sessions on infidelity, drug abuse, neglect ...

I realised I was almost at Heidi's shop and decided to drop in. I was busting to tell someone about my encounter with Kelly and I knew Heidi would be sympathetic. Rufus sat obediently outside the door on only the second try, and I went inside.

Toy Stories was a children's book-and-toyshop combined. Heidi owned and ran it—with great enthusiasm and a kind of infectious joy that guaranteed her customers left with a smile and a new adventure waiting for them between the pages of some book she'd recommended, or with hours of fun ahead playing with the perfect toy she'd found on her crowded shelves.

It was a bright, colourful place, much like Heidi herself. Today her blond hair was in its usual plaits on each side of her head, which on anyone else over the age of about nine probably would have looked silly, but it suited her perfectly. She had on a blue pinafore dress with a happy yellow T-shirt underneath. She looked exactly right amongst the rainbow of toys and colourful books that filled her shop.

"Hi there!" she said with a welcoming smile. "How's my favourite photographer?"

"Well," I began, "funny you should ask ..." and I unloaded the whole story on her.

She was a very receptive audience, gasping in shock and frowning in indignation at all the right places. When I finished up with my parting shot at Kelly, she burst out laughing and actually clapped.

"Oh, that's perfect," Heidi said. "She'll hate you forever now, but it will be worth it. I wish I could have seen her face."

"She'll probably hate me forever anyway," I said. "In fact, she seemed to hate me before she'd even met me, which hardly seems fair."

"I think Kelly's an unhappy person," Heidi said. Trust Heidi to see it so charitably.

"I *thought* that was Rufus outside," Andrea said as she entered the shop. "Hello, you two. Who are we talking about?"

Andrea was older than us—almost forty-three, in fact, since her birthday was fast approaching. I hoped Nick had found that book for her. I liked Andrea. She was smart and funny, and had an unshakeable air of calm, as if she was so comfortable in her own skin that dramas just washed over her. Maybe that came with age, or maybe that was just Andrea.

She was wearing her usual librarian "uniform" of jeans and a green button-up shirt, her dark hair swept back into a loose bun. She eyed us expectantly through her black-rimmed glasses.

"Kelly Parmenter." Heidi gave her the condensed version of my encounter on the beach.

Andrea's eyebrows rose higher through the telling, then she laughed as Heidi delivered the final line. "Nice insult. I'm proud of you."

I was starting to feel a little guilty about it. I wasn't

usually rude to people, but Kelly had gotten under my skin.

"Do *you* think she's unhappy?" I asked.

Andrea snorted. "What's she got to be unhappy about? She looks like a goddess, she has bucketloads of money, and I hear she has a new rich boyfriend. No, her problem is that she's a witch with a capital B. Don't give her another moment's thought. Did you hear about the drama at the gym?"

"What drama?" Heidi asked.

"One of our members was murdered."

"You mean Sam Middleton?" I asked.

"So you *have* heard."

"And apparently one of the staff is the prime suspect," Heidi added.

"News travels fast around here," Andrea said.

"What do you think of Kai?" I asked. "Do you think he could have done it?"

Andrea shrugged. "I like him. He's an excellent trainer. A bit quiet, maybe, but in that intense way, not as if he hasn't got two brain cells to rub together."

"Nick thinks he could be on steroids," I said.

She laughed. "Nick just says that because he's jealous of the guy's physique. You should see him. He's got a full sleeve tattoo and he looks like he could be a hitman for the Chinese mob, but he has a nice smile."

"Is he Chinese?" Heidi asked, leaning her elbows on the counter.

"Vietnamese, I think. At least, we had a conversation once about his travels there."

"He sounds intimidating," I said. "Do you think he's strong enough to kill a fit woman like Sam?"

"Of course," Andrea said immediately. "Let's face it, most men could kill a woman pretty easily."

"Dave could make mincemeat of me with one hand tied behind his back," Heidi said.

I laughed. "As if he would. He thinks the sun shines out of you."

"As he should," Andrea said, nodding gravely.

"True," I said. "You guys are so good together."

Dave was a hands-on father as well as an attentive spouse, but even when he was with their boys, he always had half an eye on his wife. You could tell she was the centre of his world.

Heidi started fussing with odds and ends on the counter. "Oh, hush. We're no different to any other married couple."

"Trust me," Andrea said, "my marriage was *nothing* like yours. If I found a man who looked at me the way Dave looks at you, I might even be tempted to try the holy state of matrimony again. And that's saying something."

Maybe one day I'd find someone like that for myself. Not for ages, of course; I wasn't ready for another relationship yet. I dreaded getting back into the dating scene. It had been years since I'd had a "first date" with anyone.

Breakfast with Curtis didn't count. That hadn't been a real date, just a couple of friends getting together. We'd chatted about a million different things—he was very easy to talk to. He'd told me all about his kayaking, and promised to take me out on the water one day. He'd told me funny stories about Maisie, and about working on the police force. I could have sat and listened to his deep voice all morning, but he'd also worked to draw me out and made me feel as if I was the most interesting person he'd ever spoken to. I'd felt myself blossoming under the warmth of his attention.

But it definitely hadn't been a date, so why, when I thought about finding a man who looked at me the way Dave looked at Heidi, had it been Curtis's dark eyes that immediately sprung to mind?

CHAPTER 9

L<small>ATE ON</small> W<small>EDNESDAY AFTERNOON</small>, R<small>UFUS AND</small> I <small>WERE OUT FOR A</small> walk. I'd been sitting at the computer all day and needed to stretch my legs, so I let Rufus range ahead and simply followed wherever he chose to go. Before I knew it, I was almost at Sam's house. Her neighbour was out watering her front garden again. She was out there so often it was a wonder the plants didn't drown.

"Hello," I said to her, stopping on the pavement outside her house. Maybe I could get some useful information from her. "I'm sorry, I didn't introduce myself the other day. I'm Charlie. And you are—?"

She squinted at me, without any sign of recognition. "Annette."

"We met before," I added. "I came over with Jess." I gestured at Sam's house, which was still cordoned off with police tape. "When we went ... when we found ..."

She moved closer, shutting the hose off. "Oh, yes. You

were there when they found the body, weren't you? What did she die of?"

"I don't know," I said, repelled by the hunger for gossip in her face. "I didn't actually see anything."

"Where was she found? Did she have clothes on?"

"She was fully dressed," I said firmly. I honestly wasn't sure if she'd been clothed or not, but I refused to give this woman more grist for the rumour-mill. "But I really didn't see much. I was too busy helping Jess."

"Oh, yes. Poor girl. It must have been very traumatic for her."

"Yes. It was. I suppose it's upsetting for you, too. You and Sam must have been friends?"

She snorted. "Hardly. After all I did for her when she moved in, too. All I wanted was for her to take down that awful tree before it killed someone, but she wouldn't have a bar of it. I haven't spoken to her in two years."

"What awful tree?"

The jacaranda in the middle of Sam's front yard was in full bloom, its soft purple flowers making a beautiful carpet on the grass beneath it. Another, taller tree stood at the side of the house, closer to the fence line. I didn't know what kind it was, but it didn't look *awful*. It was a perfectly pleasant tree—brown bark, green leaves, the usual. I couldn't see anything objectionable about it.

"That one." She jerked her head at it, anger on her face. "One day one of those nuts is going to kill someone. I *told* her that but she ignored me. Said I could pay to trim the branches that hung over the fence if I wanted to."

"Nuts?" Maybe Annette was nuts, because I couldn't

see anything that looked like it could kill someone—just some round things up high about the size of my thumbnail.

She waved angrily in the tree's direction. "The wind blows them all over my driveway. *Not* just from the branches that hang over the fence, as I told her. And they're so treacherous underfoot, my daughter Grace nearly broke her ankle. One day someone's going to slip and hit their head on the concrete, and then where will she be?" She seemed to recall belatedly that Sam was dead and wouldn't be anywhere in this hypothetical scenario. "Well, I'm sorry she came to a bad end, but it wasn't right, the way she treated me."

"I'm sorry to hear that," I said soothingly. "I guess the house will be sold now. Perhaps you'll have better luck with the new owners."

"And perhaps that tree will come over sick and die in the meantime," she said ominously. "A copper nail in the right place will work wonders, I've heard."

Wow. That seemed harsh. Poor tree—the whole thing seemed a fuss about nothing. Certainly nothing that justified tree-icide.

"So ... if you two weren't friends, I guess you don't know if there was anything strange going on in Sam's life." I left the challenge hanging in the air between us, hoping she'd take the bait.

"Well," she said, snapping it up eagerly, "there was that tattooed type she was seeing."

"Kai?"

She waved her hand dismissively. "I don't know his

name. Asian man, looked as though cracking a smile might kill him. I used to see him sometimes leaving her house early in the morning."

"Did they seem happy together?"

"I don't think I ever saw them together. Heard them, though." She nodded significantly.

"Fighting, you mean?"

"Oh, yes. Used to go at it hammer and tongs. Grace reckons they must have liked making up, because they were always yelling at each other."

"Did you see Kai leaving on Friday morning?"

"No. She kicked him out the night before. Heard them yelling, as usual, so I looked out the window. He went flouncing down the path with her standing in the doorway reading him the riot act. Set him off good and proper. He kicked the letterbox so hard it ended up on its side, then roared off down the street like a bat out of hell."

"What were they fighting about?"

"Other men, probably. It was just name-calling by then, but most of their fights seemed to be about that. He didn't like her flirting with other men, and she didn't appreciate being told what to do. And used to tell him so, at the top of her lungs."

A teenaged girl with straggly blond hair came out onto the veranda. "Mum, I can't find the nasal spray."

She sounded congested and there were shadows under her eyes.

"Get inside and do your homework," Annette snapped. "It's probably wherever it fell out of your hand last."

"Can you come and look?"

"I said, *inside*, Grace." Annette made a shooing motion with her free hand, as if she couldn't get rid of her fast enough. As if the kid were some celebrity she wanted to hide from the paparazzi. "Can't you see I'm busy?"

The girl muttered something under her breath and went back into the house, slamming the door behind her.

"Your daughter?" I asked.

"Yes. Never puts anything away then wonders why she can't find it again later."

"She doesn't look well," I said, feeling sorry for the teen. Her mother wasn't exactly Florence Nightingale. "She's got dark rings under her eyes."

"Oh, she's always got those," Annette said dismissively. "Stays up half the night chatting to her friends on Instagram or Snapchat or whatever the latest thing is. I've tried taking her phone away, but she just waits until I'm asleep and goes and gets it. I've given up. If she wants to walk around all day like a zombie, that's on her. I keep telling her if she doesn't study she'll end up like that floozy next door, but will she listen? Of course not."

I blinked. Had she really just called Sam a floozy? "You're worried she'll be murdered if she doesn't study?"

Annette gave me a look that clearly suggested I was missing a few brain cells. "No, I mean like how she was before she died."

I could feel my hackles going up, but I was determined to wring every last drop of information out of this unpleasant woman. "And how was that?"

"You know. Bringing different men home every week. Spending all her money on clothes and clubbing."

She'd just described the dream life of plenty of teenage girls. If she thought that telling Grace she'd end up like Sam if she didn't pay attention at school was going to make Grace want to study, she needed to brush up on her parenting skills.

Besides, what was wrong with spending money? Or going out with a bunch of different guys? At least Sam had seemed happy, which, I was rapidly concluding, Annette was not. I made a last-ditch effort to bring the conversation around to something more relevant.

"When you saw her last Friday morning, did she seem upset? You said she'd had a fight with Kai the night before." I wanted to ask if she was injured, but hesitated to give the woman any ideas. Before I knew it, there'd be a new rumour circulating.

Annette shrugged. "I don't know. I only saw her for a second."

I remembered Sam's text to her boss about the migraine. "Did she look as though she had a headache?"

Again I got the look questioning the number of brain cells I had. "What do headaches look like?"

Rufus, who had flopped at my feet some time ago, chose that moment to sigh heavily. *I know how you feel, buddy.*

"I was watering the roses," Annette said. "I didn't pay that much attention—I only glanced at her. She seemed fine, not upset that I could tell. Just got in her car."

"Did she say anything?"

Annette snorted scornfully. "She hadn't spoken to me in two years, she wasn't about to start then."

"What was she wearing?"

"I don't know. As I said, I only glanced at her. Jeans, I think."

"Was that normal?"

She paused, frowning at the droplets of water on the hydrangeas. "No. I suppose that was unusual. She usually wore skirts on workdays. And she had a cap on. A pink one."

I nodded. That would be the one she'd worn for the photo shoot. Jess had a matching one. "And she got in the car and drove away? Which direction did she go?"

"Down towards Beach Road. Wouldn't be much point going the other way, would there? You can't get out that way." She narrowed her eyes at me. "Why are you asking all these questions, anyway? I've already told the police everything I know."

"I'm a friend," I said. Not precisely true, but it wasn't a lie, either. And I didn't really have a better answer, anyway. It wasn't that I didn't trust the police to do a good job, but ... Detective McGovern. From my previous experience with him, he didn't strike me as a man who cared deeply about the victims and their families.

He would have kittens if he knew I was asking questions about his case, but I'd sort of gotten into the habit now. It was that sense of justice again. I just wanted to see things made right.

CHAPTER 10

RUFUS AND I HEADED BACK TOWARDS BEACH ROAD. WE'D BEEN out for a while, and my stomach was telling me it was time to start thinking about dinner. But we'd only just turned the corner when a cute little brown-and-white spaniel darted across the road and came to sniff and wag around Rufus.

Rufus was perfectly happy to make a new friend and they sniffed each other's nether regions with great interest, but I frowned at the newcomer.

"Are you supposed to be out by yourself?"

The way he—or she—had darted across the road without looking made me feel that this wasn't a habitual roamer like Rufus. This dog had no street-smarts.

I patted the dog and it looked up at me. Something about it looked familiar.

"Do I know you?"

The dog was more interested in Rufus than in me, and tried to go back to the sniff-fest, but I grabbed its collar, hoping for a tag with a name and phone number. No such luck, but the feeling that I'd seen the dog before was growing, tickling at my memory.

Then it came to me. This was Lauren's dog. She'd been taking it for a walk when she saw the cop cars outside Sam's house and stopped, only to discover her best friend had been murdered.

"Oh, dear. I really don't think you should be out by yourself." As if Lauren wasn't having a bad enough week already. Losing her dog on top of losing her best friend would be a terrible blow. "I think you'd better come with us."

Thankfully, Lauren had pointed out her house, so I knew where to take the little adventurer. He—I checked, and it was definitely a he—was happy enough to trot along with us, and I was soon knocking on Lauren's front door, hoping she was home. If I put the dog into the back yard, there was no guarantee that he wouldn't escape again.

But I needn't have worried. The door soon opened and then Lauren was on her knees, hugging her dog. "Benson! Where have you been, you bad boy?" She looked up at me. "It's not like him to wander off. Where was he?"

"Just round the corner. He hadn't gone far."

She stood up. "Thank you for bringing him home. He's got no idea about traffic at all."

"I figured." I hesitated. "So ... how are you? Are you doing okay?"

She sighed. "Not really. It's such a shock. She was my best friend."

"I'm so sorry. It must be devastating." I tried to imagine how I would have felt if it had been Amy. Back when we were friends, it would have been like losing a family member. Now, of course, I'd be just as inclined to throw a party. I still had a lot of unresolved anger where Amy was concerned.

But Lauren's situation was very different. She nodded, tears springing to her eyes. "She was always there for me. She helped me through some awful things. The whole IVF experience would have been unbearable without her—and then when the money ran out and we had to give up on IVF it was even worse." A single tear escaped and trickled down her cheek. "She checked up on me every day. Cooked meals for me. She was always ready to listen. We were going to be best friends forever. It's just so hard to believe that she's gone."

"I'm sorry," I said again helplessly. "I didn't mean to upset you."

She swiped at the tear and shook her head. "It's okay. I'm still going to think about her all the time, even if nobody mentions her. It almost helps to talk about it."

"When was the last time you saw her?"

"Oh, I don't know. I talked to her on Thursday night from my hotel—I think I saw her the day before I left for the conference? So Wednesday. Yes, it must have been, because it was at the gym. We were talking about sausages, can you believe that? What a stupid trivial thing. And even that was interrupted by Kai, as usual. He couldn't stand for her to pay attention to anyone but him. Just because he was finished work and he wanted to take her out, he kept looking at his watch and sighing. As if it was the biggest imposition in the world for her to actually talk to her best friend."

"So they *were* together?"

She shrugged. "It was more of a friends-with-benefits arrangement. They tried to keep it on the down-low. Sam wasn't serious about him. But he was possessive of her. Whenever he was around he was always trying to separate her from other people and keep her all to himself."

"How did Sam feel about that?"

"I think she was flattered. She just laughed it off whenever I tried to talk to her about it. But I was worried. They fought a lot and he's a strong guy. Very strong. He had a pretty short fuse, too. Any little thing could set him off."

I was hearing such different things about Kai. Andrea had said he was quiet, but both Annette and Lauren insisted he was always fighting with Sam. Perhaps his persona at the gym was very different to how he behaved when he and Sam were alone. "What kind of things did they fight about?"

"Stupid little things. Where they were going for dinner. The clothes she wore. He liked being in control, and he'd go off if she was even a few minutes late to meet him—and Sam was often late. He made it sound like he was doing it for her, to encourage her to be a better person. He was just a basic personal trainer, but he acted like he was some kind of motivational speaker. Told her she had to show up for herself, take her training seriously."

And then he kissed her in the men's change room despite risking his job, according to Nick. Sounded like he needed to take his own advice.

"How long ago did their relationship start?"

"I guess they met a couple of months ago when he started at the gym, but they didn't start seeing each other straight away. Five or six weeks, I guess."

She leaned against the doorjamb, as if she needed something to hold her up. The dark circles under her eyes suggested she hadn't been sleeping well since Sam died and I felt a great welling of sympathy. Thank goodness I'd caught Benson before anything had happened to him. She didn't look as though she could stand any more blows this week.

"And how long were you and Sam friends?"

She shook her head, a faraway look in her eyes. "Forever. We met on the first day of school. I was crying because I'd dropped my biscuit on the ground, so she gave me one of hers, and we've been friends ever since. We always shared everything." A cloud crossed her face.

"I'm sorry. It must be so hard. Jess told me you guys were close. She said you gave each other lottery tickets every birthday and always used the same numbers."

"She told you about that?" I nodded and she looked away, visibly upset.

"I suppose you picked numbers that meant something to you?"

"Yeah. That was Sam's idea. She was such an optimist."

"It's always nice to dream, isn't it?"

"Yeah. We started doing that in high school, when we didn't have the money for expensive presents, and it just became a tradition. Sam said it was the biggest present in the world, because it was the gift of a dream."

And now Sam's dream would never come true.

Rufus had started pacing up and down the short pathway from the gate to her front door, giving me meaningful looks over his shoulder every so often.

She straightened up. "Anyway, your dog is looking impatient. I'd better let you get going."

I laughed. "They don't need to be able to talk to tell us what they want, do they?"

She smiled down at Benson, sitting primly by her feet as if he would never dream of doing anything so naughty as running away. "This one rules the roost here. Whatever he wants, he gets. He's like my baby."

She shooed him inside, getting ready to close the door.

"Before you go," I said. "Can I ask one more thing? Do you know anything about a fight between Sam and her next-door neighbour?"

"That awful woman! She was always upset about something. Sam couldn't do anything without setting her off. What did she tell you?"

"She said they'd had a dispute about a tree. She wanted it cut down and Sam wouldn't do it."

Lauren rolled her eyes. "That tree was just the last straw. I bet she didn't tell you that she'd rung the police once a week without fail for months to complain about the noise at Sam's place. She must have hearing like a bat, because Sam only had to *think* about turning on the radio and that cow would be hammering on the door, telling her to turn it down. And then she started wittering on about the nuts on that stupid tree. The way she went on about it, you'd think they were grenades, ready to blow her house sky-high. She acted as if it was only a matter of time before someone died. From nuts! Can you believe it? What a madwoman."

"She seemed to think someone would slip on one of the nuts and have a fall."

"She's just lazy. She hated having to sweep up the leaves from that tree. She's so proud of that garden of hers, as if it's anything special. As if a few random leaves from someone else's tree could spoil its perfection. I mean, that's what trees *do*. It's nature. She told Sam that if anything happened to one of her family, she'd make sure Sam paid."

That sounded ominous. "What did Sam say?"

She shrugged. "She laughed in her face. Stupid old woman."

CHAPTER 11

T<small>HE NEXT MORNING</small>, I <small>HEARD</small> N<small>ICK WORKING AWAY AGAIN NEXT</small> door, so I went outside after breakfast to check on the progress of Jack's new deck. There were posts in the holes now, standing tall with the extra space around them filled in by wet cement. Nick was using a circular saw to cut lengths of thick timber. They looked like they would form the support for the planks of the deck.

"Hi," he said when he looked up. "Where's your friend today?"

My friend? I was confused until he glanced at the hole under the fence and I realised he meant Rufus. "He's still eating breakfast. He'll be out in a moment." I hadn't quite believed Nick when he said the deck would only take a few days, but it was coming along much more quickly than I'd expected, considering he was only one guy working alone. "I've just made a pot of coffee. Would you like some?"

"No, thanks. Had one before I started. Hope I didn't wake you?"

"No. Rufus makes sure I get up early."

"Well, I'll be done with the sawing soon. After that it'll be less noisy." He added the piece he'd just cut to a pile of similar lengths then contemplated the pile that were still to be trimmed. He removed his cap and ran a hand through his sandy blond hair before replacing it. "Did you hear the police found some fingerprints in that murder case?"

"No, I didn't. I knew they were checking, though. Everyone who'd been in the house had to get fingerprinted so they could be eliminated."

He frowned. "Oh. No, not in the house. I'm talking about the car. They identified two sets of prints on the car. And one of them was Kai's."

"Is that so unexpected? If they were seeing each other, they probably rode in each other's cars." He looked disappointed by my reaction, as if he'd expected to shock and amaze me with the news. So I made an effort to be more intrigued. "Whose were the other prints?"

"I don't know. I only know they found Kai's because the police turned up at the gym again and arrested him."

"*Arrested* him?" Now I was as shocked as he could possibly hope for. "On what grounds? Did they charge him with murder already?"

That seemed to be putting a lot of faith in a set of prints. They must have other information we didn't know about.

"No. They arrested him because he lost his temper and tried to take a swing at one of them."

"Wow. That was stupid."

Nick grinned. "I told you, this guy has a hair-trigger temper. It was quite the scene. They'll be talking about it at the gym for weeks."

"Were you there? What happened?"

He gave up any pretence of working and wandered over to the fence. "Yep. I'd just finished my workout and was chatting to Andrea before I got changed when the police arrived. They went straight over to Kai and said they had a few more questions for him and was there somewhere private they could talk?

'I already answered your questions,' he says, like a grumpy two-year-old.

'Well, we found your fingerprints on Ms Middleton's car, and we'd like to have a word.

'Of course my fingerprints are on the car,' he yells, only with a couple of f-bombs thrown in. 'We went out to dinner on Thursday night and she drove.'

'There's no need to get upset, Mr Nguyen. These are just routine questions. We have to ask you.'

'Oh, yeah?' he says, getting all up in their faces. Andrea and I couldn't believe it. 'This is harassment,' he kept saying. 'You people are trying to get me sacked, turning up here and hurling accusations around.'

'We're not hurling accusations, Mr Nguyen, we're just asking you some questions.'

"But he wasn't having a bar of it. He just kept yelling about harassment, and this one cop kept trying to ask him where he was on the morning of Friday the second, and he lost it completely."

"So they've figured out that Sam died on the Friday?" I asked.

"I guess so."

That meant she'd already been dead when Jess and I had turned up at her house on Saturday morning. The thought made me sad.

"Go on. You said he lost it?"

"He yells, 'This is because I'm Vietnamese and have tattoos, isn't it?' and then he's accusing them of setting him up and not doing their jobs properly and the next thing he starts throwing punches.

"What did the police do?" I asked.

"They had handcuffs on him faster than you can say *harassment*. I think everyone in the gym was watching by then. We've never had excitement like it."

"I wonder what the answer to that question is, though. Where *was* he the morning Sam died?"

"Oh, that's easy," he said. "He's told everyone in the gym by now, I think. According to him, he was at home asleep after their big night out the night before, and then he got in to work about midday for his shift."

"Hmmm," I said.

Nick laughed. "Exactly. No alibi. Maybe that's why he's so angry. He must know it looks bad for him."

The back door opened, revealing Jack in the doorway, dressed in blue scrubs. Nick had already removed the set of steps to make way for the deck construction, so Jack jumped down to the ground and came over to us.

"Hi," he said.

"You look tired," I said. "Have you just got home from work?"

He grimaced. "Yep. Gotta love night shift. Thought I'd come out and check on our grand project before I hit the sack."

"It's not all that grand yet," Nick said. "I've got to let the cement harden before I go any further, but I've been cutting everything to size while I wait."

Jack eyed the circular saw with misgiving. "Is that noisy?"

"Yes, but I'm nearly done, then you can get some sleep."

"Want some coffee while you wait?" I asked. "I've got a fresh pot."

"Ordinarily I'd say yes, but I'll never get to sleep if I have coffee now."

He looked so tired I thought he could probably have drunk a bucketful of coffee and still fallen asleep the minute his head hit the pillow, but he knew his own body best. Thank goodness I'd never had to do shift work. I'd be the world's grumpiest person without a regular sleep schedule, but Jack somehow managed to remain cheerful and friendly.

"It's looking really good," he said, turning to admire the bones of the deck. "I can see it already. It's going to be great to have somewhere to sit outside."

"You could have parties out here," I said.

He smiled. "I've been thinking of having a house-warming party. We could christen the deck at the same time. You're both invited, of course."

Sherlock appeared in the open doorway and surveyed the building work disdainfully. He was all black except for white socks and the tip of his tail, and his eyes were a vivid green. He was one of the prettiest cats I'd ever seen.

He leapt down with sinuous grace and stalked over to Jack, giving Nick a wide berth. Jack bent down to pat him, and he rubbed his cheek against the leg of Jack's scrubs.

"That would be fun," I said. "I thought about having a housewarming myself, but I got busy and never quite got around to it."

I didn't mention that a lot of my busyness had been because I was involved in various murder cases. My start in this neighbourhood had definitely been eventful.

"We should join forces," Jack said, "and have a joint housewarming. You invite your friends and I'll invite mine. That would be good, actually, since I don't have that many friends. I can borrow some of yours." He grinned at me, pleased with the idea.

"You must have heaps of friends," I protested. He seemed so open and friendly—how could people resist his easy charm?

"Well, of course I've got plenty of mates in Brisbane. But I'm new around here. The only people I know are other nurses and you guys." He picked up the cat and stroked his sleek fur. "And it's harder to make friends when you're a shift worker, isn't it, Sherlock?"

Sherlock meowed and headbutted Jack's chin. Jack was still smiling, but I sensed loneliness under the laughter and instantly I wanted to wrap him up in a warm

Sunny Bay welcome and fill his house with all the lovely people I'd met here.

"But how would a joint housewarming work? If we didn't have a fence here it would be one thing, but I don't think my landlord would be thrilled at us taking down his fence."

"You could make it like a progressive dinner," Nick said.

"What's a progressive dinner?" I asked.

Nick rolled his eyes and muttered something about young people under his breath, even though he was probably only ten years older than me.

"It's a dinner party where each course takes place at a different house. So one house hosts the first course, another hosts the second, and someone else does the dessert, and all the guests travel between the houses for each course."

That sounded like an odd arrangement. It would mean half the guests wouldn't be able to drink, as they'd either be cooking or behind the wheel. Maybe that was why I hadn't heard of one before—they'd probably fallen out of favour when the drink-driving laws were introduced. I'd have to ask Aunt Evie if she'd ever been to one.

"That sounds perfect," Jack said, and I nodded, getting excited. There'd be no problem with drink-driving, since people would only have to walk a few steps from my front door to his. "I can host a barbecue here on the deck, and then we can all move next door to yours for dessert."

"That seems like a lot more work for you," I said, a little doubtfully.

"Not at all," he said. "I'll just throw some sausages on the barbie and whip up a big salad. Too easy."

"Okay." I grinned back at him. His enthusiasm was infectious. "I'll invite all my book club friends."

"Ah, the famous book club! What do you read?"

"Only books by dead people. Why? Are you interested in joining?"

"Could be. There are plenty of dead sci-fi authors. Might be a bit hard to make meetings, though, with shift work."

"Well, we can work something out. It would be nice for you to meet them, at least. When do you want to do this?"

"No time like the present. Saturday?"

"The day after tomorrow?" I squeaked.

"Why not? If we leave it much longer, everyone will be going to Christmas parties. Is Saturday a problem for you?"

"I guess not." I was warming to the idea. I'd done so many spontaneous things lately. What was a little party compared to moving to a new town and starting a business?

"Nick?"

"I'm free," Nick said.

"Great. Let's do this!" Jack yawned hugely, only half-covering it with his hand. "Sorry. Right, well, now that's settled, I'm off to bed."

CHAPTER 12

"So," I said the next day. "Do you think a man could join our book club?"

Heidi gave me a knowing sort of half-smile. "Do you have someone in mind?"

I'd dropped into Toy Stories to invite Heidi to the party. Behind the counter, in pride of place on the wall, was a massive canvas of a photo I'd taken myself in my first ever shoot as a professional photographer. In it, her twins Noah and Zach leapt off a boulder, arms thrown out in glee, with a glorious sky behind them that was as blue as the cute little dress Heidi was wearing today. That one photo had brought me most of my business so far, as customers invariably asked who the photographer was, and Heidi always replied by shoving one of my business cards into their hands and singing my praises to the heavens.

Heidi had been my first real friend here in Sunny Bay, and she'd almost singlehandedly restored my faith in humanity after my last "best friend" turned out to be anything but. I often stopped into the shop when I was in town just to say hello.

"My new neighbour," I said, and her smile faded. I knew she'd assumed I was talking about Curtis—she was very keen to shove me into the arms of Sunny Bay's most eligible policeman. I supposed it came from enjoying such a happy marriage herself—she was an incurable romantic, and was always eager for others to experience that same happiness.

But in a moment she'd adapted and the smile was back. Not that Heidi ever stopped smiling for long. It was built into her DNA.

"Your new neighbour? Tell me more—is he single?"

"I think so." I'd assumed there was no girlfriend, given what he'd said about not knowing many people in the area, but I could have been way off. "He's just moved here from Brisbane. I guess there could be someone waiting for him back there, but I don't think so."

"Good. How old is he? Does he seem nice?"

"Don't know. Late twenties, early thirties? And yes, very nice." I held up my hand. "But before you start planning my wedding, can we get back to the original question? Do you think our club would be open to the idea of having a man join?"

"I don't see why not." She tidied piles of books and cards on the counter as she spoke. Heidi was always in motion. It probably came from being the mother of five-year-old twins. "We're always happy to have new members."

"I just wondered if it was meant to be women only."

"No. We never discussed anything like that. I think it was only that Peggy didn't know any men who liked reading the classics."

Peggy had founded the book club before I'd moved to Sunny Bay. I'd met her a few times when I'd visited Aunt Evie, back when I still lived in Sydney. Sadly, she'd been murdered the same week I'd moved in permanently, so I never got to see her in action at the book club. She'd been a lady who loved a good chat, a kind of older, slowed-down version of Heidi.

"Okay. I'll let Jack know." I got out some more of my business cards and added them to the holder Heidi kept them in by the cash register. "And speaking of Jack—he and I are having a joint housewarming party on Saturday night. Are you and Dave free? I know it's not a lot of notice, but Jack doesn't know many people and I thought it would be nice to introduce him around a bit."

"I'll check with Dave's mum and see if she can babysit the boys. It shouldn't be a problem. What would you like me to bring?"

I grinned. "Just Dave. Jack and I will handle the catering. It'll be a very casual dinner."

"How are you going to housewarm both houses? Or is it just at your place?"

I told her Jack's plan, which earned her approval. She clapped her hands with typical Heidi enthusiasm. "A progressive dinner! My parents used to go to those when I was a kid. The church used to organise them. I haven't heard of anyone doing one in years."

"Well, we're bringing them back into style."

"I never thought I'd get to go to one."

"There you go. You can tick that one off your bucket list. Jack and I are making the eighties cool again. Or was it the seventies?"

"You know, *Jack and I* sounds rather good when you say it like that."

"Hush, you! I'm not interested in Jack."

Heidi fiddled with a pile of books on the counter and asked, rather too casually, "So ... is Curtis coming to this party?"

"I haven't invited him."

She formed the books into a neat stack. "Why not?"

I shrugged. "I know your little matchmaking brain is working overtime here, but there's nothing going on between us."

"Uh-huh." She paused. "So you're just friends."

"Right."

"Then why not invite him?"

"Because ..." I straightened the perfectly straight business cards in their little stand. "No reason. I just ... haven't."

"You haven't." That was her mum voice, patently disbelieving. "You're having a party for all your *friends*, but you haven't invited one of them."

"Okay, fine. I'm nervous."

"About what?"

"I ... don't want him to get the wrong idea."

She rolled her eyes. "Charlie, it's perfectly obvious that the man has plenty of *ideas* where you're concerned already. Nothing you do or don't do will change that. And if he's your friend, you should invite him."

"You're right. You're right." Not about Curtis having ideas—surely he would have asked me out again already if that was the case—but that I should invite all my friends. I didn't have so many that I could afford to leave anyone out. I caught her satisfied grin and frowned at her. "You're even more of a matchmaker than Priya's mother."

She laughed. "Poor Priya. Amina is really pulling out all the stops on this one. Now she's got Rakesh trying to persuade Priya as well."

Rakesh was Priya's younger brother. I'd met him recently; he was about twenty-five and single himself. "What a traitor! He'd better be careful or his mother will start planning *his* future. I'm surprised he'd get involved."

"I don't think Amina gave him a choice. He probably went along with it so she'd harass Priya instead of him."

"I knew Priya didn't mean all that stuff she said at book club that time about how people had just as much chance of being happy in an arranged marriage as they did in one where they'd picked their own partner."

Now that it had come down to it, arranged marriages weren't looking so inviting to her. I did feel sorry for her, though. She loved her mum and generally tried to please her—within reason. But this was where she'd drawn the line, and the conflict wouldn't be making either of them happy.

In contrast, Aunt Evie, who was the closest thing I had to a mum, had never interfered in my love life—even though, as I'd recently discovered, she'd never liked Will at all and had thought he would make me a terrible husband. And how right she was. Maybe she *should* have interfered. It would have saved me wasting years of my life on him.

But in all honesty, I probably wouldn't have listened— and then I'd have been mad at her for sticking her oar in. Smart woman.

I rang her as I headed home.

"Hello, darling," she said. "What's up?"

"I'm just ringing to say I love you."

She laughed. "Why, what have you done?"

"Aunt Evie! Don't be so cynical. I was just thinking about how good you are and I wanted to tell you."

Her voice filled with warm pleasure. I could tell she was smiling. "Thank you, darling. I love you, too. And now I'm wondering what *I've* done?"

"Nothing. Just been yourself. Oh, also—what are you doing on Saturday night?"

"Nothing, why?"

"I'm having a joint housewarming party with my new neighbour, Jack." I filled her in on the details and she promised to come "with bells on".

By then I was home. Rufus gave me a rapturous welcome, implying that I'd been gone for several weeks instead of half an hour and suggesting that a dog needed a lot of pats and maybe one of his special treats to make up for such gross neglect. Then he settled himself on my feet while I made some more phone calls, inviting everyone from my book club to come to the housewarming.

I looked at Curtis's number in my phone. I should call him, but despite Heidi's reassurances, I hesitated. I wasn't interested in chasing a guy who wasn't keen—I'd just finished one disastrous relationship and I figured that next time I'd do it right. I'd make sure I found a guy who truly appreciated me and wasn't secretly checking out my friends behind my back.

Not that I thought Curtis would do such a thing. He was no Will. But if he wasn't all in, I wasn't either, even if my heart rate spiked whenever I saw him. Any straight woman with a pulse would feel *something* when faced with that slow, sweet smile and those gorgeous dark eyes. It wasn't *my* fault that God had made him so handsome it was practically a sin.

In fact, it was probably a *good* thing that he hadn't taken things any further. I had the feeling it would be too easy to fall hard for a man like Curtis, and my wounded heart needed more time to heal before I threw it back in the arena. Keeping a little distance from Officer Kane was the sensible thing to do in the circumstances.

But surely a girl could invite her friend to a party.

My phone started ringing in my hand, and I jumped. Rufus gave me a grumpy look; my little squeak of surprise had disturbed him.

Speak of the devil. It was Curtis.

CHAPTER 13

"HI," I SAID, HOPING I DIDN'T SOUND AS BREATHLESS AS I FELT.

"Hi," he said. "It's Curtis."

I shook my head. It was kind of touching that he didn't think I would have his name saved in my phone. Someone who looked like he did ought to be used to having women fall all over him.

Maybe being married to a supermodel made you feel ugly.

I cleared my throat. "Hi, Curtis," *Try to sound normal.* "How are you?" What did normal sound like, anyway?

"I'm ... good." The hesitation made me think he wasn't good at all. "I was ringing to ask you a favour, actually."

"Sure." *Okay, if you can't manage normal, at least be cool.* "What's up?"

"I heard you met Kelly the other day."

"Yeah." Was that the problem? Or was he just working his way around to the problem? "She was with Maisie on the beach."

"I had a phone call from Maisie just now. She was telling me about it and then she got all upset."

"Oh, no!" Poor Maisie. "What was she upset about?"

"Kelly's just left for a photo shoot in the southern highlands. Maisie is upset her mother gets to have nice photos taken of her and she doesn't. I'm not quite sure what happened, because Maisie was crying too much, but apparently you offered to let her model for you and Kelly said no?"

"Oh, the poor baby." Resentment for Kelly welled up inside me at the thought of sweet little Maisie being so upset. I should have kept my mouth shut—I *would* have, if I'd known how her mother would react to a simple offer to take a stupid photo. Was everything a commodity to be traded for money with her, even her daughter's happiness? I told Curtis what had happened and what Kelly had said about models needing to be paid. "I'm so sorry, I never meant to upset Maisie. I wasn't even talking about a photo shoot. I just said that I'd take a photo of her some time. It was just a casual offer."

Curtis sighed. "Modelling is Maisie's dream, unfortunately. She wants to be just like Mummy when she grows up. Having her photo taken is a big deal to her."

"Apparently it's a big deal to Kelly, too. I'm sorry," I repeated. I was mad, too—mad that Kelly had made Maisie so upset over something that was meant to be a nice thing. "What can I do to make it up to Maisie?"

"That's the favour I want to ask you," he said. "I was wondering if you would take some photos of Maisie. I'll pay you for your time, of course."

"But ... but Kelly said no."

"Maisie must have told her that you and I met for breakfast that time. Poor kid. If only she knew what her mother was really like, she'd realise that that was like a red flag to a bull. Kelly will do anything to get at me, even if it means Maisie gets hurt in the process." His voice hardened. "She said no just to spite me, but I don't need her permission to have a friend take photos of my own daughter. As long as you don't put them on your website or use them yourself in any way she doesn't have a leg to stand on. She can't claim that Maisie is being exploited or used as a model if you're only taking some photos to give to me." He hesitated, then added diffidently. "But I would completely understand if you said no. You probably don't want to get drawn into my dramas. Although I have to warn you, if Kelly thinks I'm interested in you, there's probably no avoiding the dramas."

I bit my lip to stop myself from asking, "So *are* you interested in me?" Instead, I took a deep breath, then said, "Of course I'll take photos of Maisie for you. But you won't be paying for them. It's just one friend doing a favour for another, right?"

There was a pause. "I don't want to be an—"

"Imposition?" I finished for him, smiling. He'd said the same thing the first time he'd come to my house with Maisie in tow and she and I had bonded over making fairy bread together. "Why do you always assume you're an imposition? Maybe I like your company." Worried that that sounded too much like a come-on, I hurried on. "*I* love taking photos of cute kids, *you* have a cute kid, it's a win-win situation. When do you want to do it?"

"I know this is short notice, but how about tomorrow? I've got Maisie for the weekend. I'll be picking her up at eight o'clock from her grandmother's house."

"Sure. Tomorrow is fine." We arranged the place and time then said goodbye. It wasn't until I'd hung up that I realised I'd forgotten to ask him to the housewarming. Never mind, I could do it tomorrow.

"That woman is a first-class witch," I said to Rufus. He twitched an ear in my direction but didn't bother raising his head from the carpet. "She's got the sweetest daughter in the world but she makes her miserable just to get at her ex-husband. Who does a thing like that?"

Rufus shifted position onto his side, stretching all four legs out straight before relaxing again. I started tidying my desk rather forcefully, trying to distract myself from the anger I felt towards Kelly. I organised my files within an inch of their lives and ruthlessly discarded photo prints I no longer needed. Fifteen minutes later, I ended up with a clear desk and a calmer mind.

Sorting through my paperwork had reminded me that I meant to ring Jess. I hadn't spoken to her since the awful day we'd discovered Sam's body together.

"How are you doing?" I asked when she picked up. "Really doing, I mean."

Too often, people said they were fine or gave some other noncommittal answer when you asked how they were, even though their world had fallen apart around them. No one treated *How are you?* as a genuine question.

It was just a social nicety to be brushed off with the expected meaningless, bland response.

"I'm doing okay," she said. "Mum and Dad flew in from Melbourne and my brother and his wife brought their kids over from Western Australia. It's nice to have everyone together."

I nodded, even though she couldn't see me. I remembered how relieved I'd been when Aunt Evie arrived the day after Mum died. Even though death is a terrible reason to get together, it does help to have family around you in the darkest moments of your life.

"I'm glad," I said. "It's easier together. There's always someone feeling strong enough to hold it together when someone else starts falling apart. You can lean on each other."

"That's right," she said. "You sound like you're speaking from personal experience."

"My mum died when I was a kid. I still miss her every day."

"Does it get better?" She sounded so lost.

I sighed. "You never stop missing them. But eventually there'll come a time when you don't think of them every day, and then a time when you can even think of them sometimes without feeling sad. Just remembering something funny they used to say, or something you did together. And there won't be the pain, just the love."

"I can't imagine that."

"I know. It's hard to believe at the beginning, when the loss is so raw. But you'll get there one day, I promise." Rufus nudged my hand with his wet nose, as if he could tell I was feeling shaky as my own memories flooded me. I patted his silky head gratefully and cleared my throat. "I was actually ringing to see if you needed a nice photo of Sam for the funeral. Free of charge, of course. I could put one of the close-ups of her in a nice silver frame for you to put on the coffin. It's one less thing for you to organise."

"Thank you. You're so thoughtful. If only there were more people in the world like you, and less who went around killing people for no reason. Sam didn't deserve to die."

"No, of course she didn't."

"I wish the police would arrest someone. Knowing that her killer is still walking around out there, free to live his life while she's dead, is awful. It's so unfair."

"I'm sure they're doing all they can. They'll want to build a good case against whoever it is, so they can be sure of a conviction."

"They found Kai's fingerprints on her car, you know."

"Yes, I heard."

"Some others, too. Some teenager who found the car abandoned and took it for a joyride."

I didn't understand why the car had been abandoned. Did the police know? It made no sense to me. Where was Sam going when she left that morning? Did she get carjacked? But why would the killer take her back to her house to kill her? Or had she been killed after she'd returned home, and the killer fled the scene in her car? Maybe Annette hadn't noticed Sam return and someone else drive the car away again. But that almost raised more questions than it answered. If you were going to steal your victim's car, why would you then abandon it only a few streets away?

I shook my head. "I thought modern cars were harder to hotwire. How does some kid know how to do it?"

"He didn't have to. The car was abandoned with the keys still in the ignition. The police found them in the bushes near where the car was found. All her keys were on that keyring—house keys as well as car keys. The only thing that was missing was the charm she kept on it—the J that we bought in New York together. It was her idea for us to swap initials. She said it was so we could always have a little piece of each other, even when we were apart." Her voice trembled and broke. "I would have liked to keep that, to remember that trip and the promises we made to each other."

"You still have the S," I said soothingly. "And the memories. No one can take those away from you."

She drew in a deep, shaky breath. "You're right. Thank you, Charlie. For everything. You're a good friend."

CHAPTER 14

THE NEXT MORNING I WAS ON THE BEACH BY EIGHT O'CLOCK, camera at the ready. Maisie was set on the idea of having her photo taken with her sandcastle, so I started digging while I was waiting, piling the sand up loosely. She'd have a good amount of sand ready to start building with when she arrived. Rufus eyed my digging with only mild interest, then headed off down the beach to find something more interesting to do.

"You could have made yourself useful," I called after him. "You dig holes in the backyard happily enough—why not here where I actually *want* you to dig?"

He ignored me, and a few minutes later a high-pitched voice shrieked my name. Curtis and Maisie had arrived.

"What are you doing?" she asked, crouching down to examine the hole I'd dug as if she thought there might be gold in the bottom.

"Digging up some prime castle-building sand for you," I said. "I reckon you should build your castle right there."

I indicated a spot behind me where the sand was still damp but not saturated and the surface had been smoothed by the waves.

"That's a good spot, Maisie Moo," Curtis said, setting down a whole construction crew's worth of buckets, spades, and various castle-shaping bits of brightly coloured plastic. He had a hot pink towel slung around his neck, and a beach bag over his shoulder. "If we dig a moat in the front there, the waves will fill it for us."

"Won't your camera get wet?" she asked, frowning at me.

"Nope." I gestured at my camera bag, which I'd left well away from the water on sand that had been dry for hours. "It will either be in there or around my neck, and I'm not planning on going swimming."

It looked as though the two of them might be. Maisie was wearing a purple-and-blue one-piece that looked like it owed its ruffled inspiration to Disney. Her bare arms and legs were a warm golden brown. Presumably Curtis had already slathered her with sunscreen, but she was so tanned she probably didn't need it at this time of day.

Curtis had on navy blue board shorts and a white T-shirt that hugged his pecs in a rather distracting way. The white showed off his own tan, which was even deeper than his daughter's, and I sighed. I'd spent most of my time in the past few years in city offices. I had some catching up to do to build a tan like these beach babes.

Maisie began carefully filling one of her sandcastle moulds with sand. After a moment she said in a very firm tone, "You can help me, Daddy."

Left in no doubt as to his role in the proceedings, Curtis grinned, showing his dimple, and got to work. He filled all the buckets and little tower- and turret-shapes with sand, leaving Maisie to the more artistic work of deciding where each one should go. She was a little tyrant, bossing us both around, hands set firmly on her non-existent hips. It made me laugh to see Curtis on his knees, scraping up sand with his big, capable hands, checking gravely with his tiny boss where each one should be deposited. In no time at all we had a big square castle with towers at the four corners, and nicely crenellated ramparts. Inside, the biggest tower rose from the centre, and Maisie found a stick to shove into the top to be the flag pole.

Then it was on to the delicate engineering work of digging the moat. Rufus returned in the middle of that and joined in enthusiastically.

"Traitor," I muttered as I sneaked off to get out my camera. Father and daughter—and wet, sandy dog— looked so adorable together, all digging away at the moat that had suddenly turned into a large lake in front of the castle.

I snapped away while they were engrossed, getting some close-ups of the adorable frown of concentration on Maisie's face, and their hands working together, her tiny ones dwarfed by his larger ones, but both sets covered in wet sand.

By this time the lake was big enough for Maisie to sit in. Rufus decided it looked like a nice cool bath and joined her, trampling all over her with his usual enthusiastic disregard for personal space. She squealed with laughter and I caught each precious moment, snapping away happily.

This was the best kind of photo shoot, where the subject was happily engaged in doing something else and barely even aware of the camera. It made for more natural shots and genuine smiles. I'd been shooting for ten minutes before Maisie looked up and told me she was ready for her photos now.

"Shall we take some with you by yourself first, and then a few with Daddy?" I asked.

"And with Rufus!" She grabbed him in a hug that was more of a headlock, but he wasn't concerned. "He's such a good dog. Why can't we have a dog like this, Daddy?"

Curtis sat back on his heels and wiped sandy hands on his white T-shirt. "You know Mummy doesn't like dogs and I do shift work. It wouldn't be fair to a dog for it to be alone in the backyard so often when I was at work."

"I could look after it," she said, rubbing her cheek against Rufus's ear.

"But you wouldn't be there much either, Maisie Moo. You're at Mummy's house most of the time, or Grandma's."

"What about if you got *two* dogs?" The kid was cunning, and the earnest look on her face was the cutest thing ever. I hid a smile as I zoomed in for a few close-ups. "Then they could look after each other."

"My backyard's too small for two dogs."

Her mouth turned down and she hid her face in

Rufus's sandy coat for a moment. "Then can we visit Charlie every weekend so I can play with Rufus?"

Curtis flicked a quick glance at me. "I would love to visit Charlie every weekend, but she has her own life."

He would? I stared at his profile and forgot to take any photos. In fact, for a moment, I almost forgot to breathe.

"But Charlie doesn't mind, do you?" She turned her little heart-shaped face to me, big brown eyes pleading.

Curtis spoke before I could answer. "Don't bother Charlie, sweetheart. You don't want her to get sick of us, do you?"

I lifted the camera to hide my face, hoping he would think the rush of heat to my cheeks was from the sun. All I could hear was Aunt Evie's voice saying, *carpe diem.*

"I'm always happy to see you both," I said. "And Rufus is, too. Now, how about we get some shots with the two of you together?"

She was immediately distracted. "Come over here, Daddy. Sit there, so Charlie can see our sandcastle."

I got some lovely shots of them but I ended the shoot before my littlest subject could get bored. She decided to paddle in the shallow water then, so Curtis and I sat side by side on the sand, watching her.

It was a beautiful day. Blue sky above, blue water below. I was sitting on a picture-perfect beach with sand between my toes, the sun warm on my skin and the scent of salt in every breath. For a moment I indulged a daydream that the gorgeous man beside me was more than a friend, and the cute little moppet in the blue and purple swimsuit was mine to cuddle and tuck into bed at night. It was all I'd ever wanted, wrapped up in one photo-genic bundle. Pure bliss.

I cleared my throat. "So ... if you're not doing anything tonight, I'm having a little housewarming party with a few friends."

"I'd love to come," he said. "But I'm working tonight."

"That's a shame." I said it lightly, surprised at how disappointed I felt.

It was easy to be sensible and say I wasn't interested in a new relationship when Curtis wasn't around, but when I was with him the idea felt a lot more tempting. It was as if I forgot how wonderful he was until I saw him again in person. Up close like this, he was overwhelming, all muscles and gorgeous chocolate-brown eyes and that heart-stopping dimple.

Such a shame that there was an ex-wife in the picture, like a snake in paradise. Maisie was hers, not mine. And while Kelly might not have a claim on Curtis anymore, at least her existence reminded me that he wasn't, in fact, perfect.

As if he knew I'd been thinking about his ex, he said, "I want to apologise to you. I'm sorry Kelly was so rude the other day."

"You don't have to apologise for her. Her behaviour is nothing to do with you."

He sighed. "As I said, she'll do anything to get at me. She's a paranoid person by nature and she only gets worse when she's using."

I glanced sideways at him. His face was stern, as if he

was used to hiding his feelings. "You think she's using now?"

"She denied it, of course, when I confronted her about it. But I'm seeing some of the same signs as last time." He turned to face me, a haunted look in his eyes. "I worry about Maisie, left alone with her. She's too young to take care of herself."

"Kelly seemed perfectly normal when I spoke to her." Not that I was as familiar with the signs of a drug addiction as a police officer would be. "Just rude."

He laughed. "Yes, that's Kelly."

I picked up a handful of sand and let it sift gently through my fingers. "But why would she be paranoid about me? I'm no threat to her."

"Either she thinks that you'll come between her and Maisie or ..." He paused, and I turned from the view to find him watching me, an almost shy expression on his face. "Or she realises how much I like you."

My eyes widened and I lost my grip on the English language so completely that all I could do was stare at him.

"I wasn't a hundred per cent straight with you the other day," he continued slowly. "When I said that I'd been too busy with work to contact you."

I looked down at my sandy feet. "You don't have to contact me if you don't want to."

"But that's the thing; I *do* want to. I'd like to get to know you better. It's just ... well, you've seen what Kelly's like. She'd be ten times worse if we were actually going out. I *have* to put up with her, but it doesn't seem fair to drag someone else into the madhouse."

My heart beat faster as I looked up and met his anxious gaze. I could get lost in those eyes. *Carpe diem.* Had I really thought I didn't want a relationship with this man? I was such an idiot sometimes.

"What if they want to be there?"

"Ah." He reached out and closed his big hand around mine, his expression changing to one of delight. The dimple peeped out again as he smiled at me. "In that case, maybe we could work something out."

I sat there, absurdly conscious of the feel of his hand— the warmth of his skin, the texture of each little grain of sand that coated it, the sheer size of it. I felt like a teenager with her first crush.

And it was the nicest feeling in the world. I couldn't remember the last time I'd been so happy.

"I'm sorry Kelly makes it so hard for you. It must be tough, being forced to deal with her all the time because of Maisie."

"I'd put up with a lot worse for Maisie's sake." He watched the little girl playing, his face alight with love.

She looked back at us and waved, too caught up in what she was doing to notice our joined hands. "Look, Charlie! I'm giving Rufus a bath." She tipped a bucket full of water over Rufus's shoulders.

"Be careful, or he'll give you one, too," I called, but I was too late. Rufus shook vigorously to rid himself of the extra water, showering Maisie with droplets. She thought it was the funniest thing she had ever seen, her shrieks of laughter competing with the harsh cries of the seagulls wheeling overhead.

"She's such a cutie," I said to Curtis. "I could eat her up."

"She is," he agreed, still with that soft look on his face, "but she's got my stubborn nature. I hate to think what she's going to be like as a teenager."

"I bet she'll still have you wrapped around her little finger."

He laughed, stroking his thumb idly along mine. "I'm not taking that bet."

"Speaking of teenagers, Jess told me that three kids found Sam's car abandoned and took it for a joy ride."

"Yeah. We're looking into that." There was an odd, cynical note in his voice.

I cocked an eyebrow at him. "You don't believe that?"

"Oh, I believe they took it for a joy ride all right. We busted them because we had the fingerprints of one of them in the system already. He's been done a couple of times for the same thing. This time he decided to set the car alight at the end of it to destroy any evidence that pointed to him. Luckily he's about as good at arson as he is at everything else and we still managed to get a good set of his prints off the car."

"What about the other kids?"

"No priors. Just a couple of stupid kids who were hanging around looking for trouble when they should have been at school. Friends of his."

"So what's the part you don't believe?"

"I don't want to say too much, since it's still under

investigation." He gave me a sidelong glance and grinned. "And I know I'm talking to Sunny Bay's most persistent detective."

I grinned back. "Don't let Detective McGovern hear you talking like that."

"I'm just not convinced they found the car where they said they did."

"I wondered about that, too," I said. "How did it get there? Who drove it—Sam or the killer? Why was Sam's body under her bed if she'd driven somewhere else?"

"Yeah, there are a lot of things that don't quite add up about this case."

"Do you know where she died? Was it in the house or somewhere else?"

"I can't tell you that, Detective Carter." He smiled at me to soften the refusal and my heart did a little skip. Had there ever been a more attractive man in the history of the universe? I was pretty sure the answer was, *no*.

And now he was sitting here, holding my hand. *Thanks, universe.*

"But you don't think those teenagers killed her, do you?"

He shrugged. "Everything is still possible. McGovern isn't ruling anything out. But since I can see you're bursting with curiosity I'll say this—people are rarely killed by strangers. I'm not saying it doesn't happen, but the statistics show that most killers are known to their victims and they're usually someone close. In the case of female victims, unfortunately in over sixty per cent of cases the killer is her spouse or ex-spouse. If Sam was married, the first person we'd be looking at would be her husband."

But since she wasn't married, that didn't bode too well for Kai. A volatile partner who she was known to fight with—even if Curtis was too professional to say so, I imagined that the surly personal trainer was on the very top of Detective McGovern's list of suspects.

CHAPTER 15

I FLOATED AROUND THE HOUSE FOR AN HOUR, HUMMING AS I tidied up for the party, bursting with an overwhelming happiness. I almost rang Aunt Evie to tell her I'd just *carped* the stuffing out of her *diem*, but in the end I decided this feeling needed time to percolate. The moment felt too fresh to share just yet.

Eventually reality intruded on my blissed-out state. I had to make two pavlovas for dessert before the guests arrived, and I had no fresh fruit and cream to decorate them with. And nowhere near enough eggs. I also wanted some decorations for the tables and maybe a few extra glasses. There was a Target in Waterloo Bay, so I decided to go there to pick up some cheap glassware and serving dishes before heading to the supermarket.

Target's car park was full, but I found a spot in the street around the corner. Waterloo Bay wasn't terribly big, so it wasn't far to walk. But when I got out of the car, I realised that Beach Bods, the gym where Kai worked, was just down the street.

I could drop in—it would only take a few minutes. *And do what? Demand Kai confess to killing Sam?* Detective McGovern would be absolutely thrilled to have me poking around in his investigation. The sensible thing to do would be to head for Target and get my shopping done so I could go home and make pavlovas.

Sensible was kind of overrated.

Before I'd had time to think better of it, my feet had carried me right to the entry of Beach Bods. I'd met Andrea and Nick outside before, but I'd never been in. The glass doors swished open at my approach, letting out a blast of air-conditioned air that smelled strongly of chlorine and more faintly of heat gel and sweat.

The floor was made of some kind of black rubbery stuff that gave slightly underfoot. High energy music was pumping from overhead speakers and past the reception area I could see a large room full of treadmills, bikes and other exercise equipment. A blond girl in bike shorts and a blue T-shirt emblazoned with the Beach Bods logo was behind the large black counter. She smiled brightly as I entered.

"Can I help you?"

For the second time that day, my brain switched off completely, leaving me staring blankly at her.

"Is, um, Kai in?" I managed at last.

The faintest of frowns appeared on her tanned forehead. "Do you have an appointment?"

Inspiration arrived in the nick of time. "No, I was

hoping he could show me around. I've been thinking of joining a gym and getting a personal trainer and a friend of mine recommended him."

"Is your friend a member here?"

"Yes." I paused. "Or, at least, she was."

She eyed me suspiciously. "What's her name?"

"Sam. Sam Middleton."

"Oh." Her eyes widened and she leaned across the desk confidentially. "Oh, honey, I'm not sure Kai is the right person to show you around. Perhaps you could come back tomorrow and I can get one of the other PTs to help you?"

That sounded like Kai was here. Excellent.

"Sam said he was the best," I insisted.

"But last week Sam asked to switch to Veronica instead." She lowered her voice. "Just before she died."

"Oh, I know all about that," I said, lying with what I considered to be impressive confidence. "I'd still rather see Kai."

"I'll just go and see if he's available," she said, giving me a still-doubtful look. "I'll be right back."

Well, that was interesting. Why had Sam requested a change of trainer? Had their fights got so bad that she wanted to dump him? But they went out for dinner on the Thursday night before she died, so that didn't make sense.

Maybe it was the other way around, and she wanted a different trainer so she and Kai could go out together with putting his job in peril. I'd have to check with Nick about that no-fraternising policy. Maybe it only applied to direct trainer-client relationships. Surely Beach Bods couldn't stop people from going out just because they occasionally used the same gym facilities?

The girl reappeared with a stocky, dark-haired guy in tow. He was wearing black shorts and the same uniform shirt that she was, but his stretched tight over a powerful chest and bared muscled arms. His left arm was covered all the way to his wrist with a full tattoo.

"Hi, I'm Kai," he said, with a smile that barely flickered across his lips before it died. His dark eyes were cool, even a little wary. "You wanted to see me?"

He wasn't much taller than me, but he moved with a swagger common in bigger men, one that suggested he knew just how strong he was. And maybe how much women liked looking at him.

"I'm Charlie," I said. "I was hoping, if you're not too busy, that you could give me a quick tour of the gym. You came highly recommended."

He glanced at his watch. "Sure. I have ten minutes before my next client. Come this way."

He led me into the big room full of treadmills and bikes. "This is our cardio room. It's open from 6am till midnight. Were you thinking of a general membership or did you have a personalised program in mind?"

"Probably a personalised program. My friend Sam recommended it."

At Sam's name, his face closed over. "What are your fitness goals?"

I babbled something about upper body strength, racking my brains. How was I going to get him to talk about something he so clearly didn't want to discuss?

He led the way into the weights room, which was filled with a bunch of unfamiliar machines that looked vaguely threatening. An older man with a red, sweaty face was using one of them, doing something that looked painful, judging by the amount of grunting that was going on. He ignored us, focusing on his own reflection in the floor-to-ceiling mirrors.

Kai talked about a couple of the machines and how they might feature in a personalised program for me. I nodded and smiled in all the right places, but I wasn't really listening.

"And would you be my trainer?" I asked as he gave me a tour of the changing facilities and explained the locker system.

"Probably one of the others would take you," he said. "My schedule is pretty full."

I knew he had at least one vacancy now that Sam was dead, but it seemed tacky to say so.

"Sam said you were the best," I said. He gave me a flat, expressionless stare. "And I know she wasn't just saying that because you were her boyfriend." There was a flicker of emotion at that. "I'm sorry for your loss," I added. "I didn't know her that well, but she was great fun."

"I didn't know her that well either," he said. "Who told you we were going out?"

"Several people. Sam's neighbour said you were there all the time."

His face twisted into a grimace. "I suppose she was complaining about the noise again."

"She did say you fought a lot. And that you were the

one who destroyed Sam's letterbox."

"Lots of people fight," he said, clenching his fists. "It doesn't mean they don't care about each other."

"Of course not," I said, putting as much sympathy into my tone as I could. "Some couples thrive on that kind of relationship. Everyone's relationship is different."

"That's right." His tone was fierce.

I took a subtle step back. He looked ready to explode. "And I'm sure you had a really good reason for the letterbox."

"I—" Suddenly, he deflated, and despair filled those dark eyes. "It's my fault she's dead. If I hadn't lost my temper and stormed out that night, I would have still been there in the morning and she wouldn't have been killed."

Clearly he'd given up on trying to convince me they hadn't been an item. "Why did you lose your temper?"

"You said yourself, everyone has different kinds of relationships, right? Well, I was kind of seeing someone else, too."

I blinked. That *was* a different kind of relationship. We were standing in a quiet corner near the change rooms and it occurred to me that he might have kissed Sam in this very spot. In between kissing someone else. "And Sam found out?"

"Yeah. She threw me out."

Good for Sam.

"And that made you so mad you smashed her letterbox?"

"No. I got mad because she was so angry with me that she threatened to tell the gym about us and get me fired."

CHAPTER 16

I THREW MYSELF INTO PARTY PREPARATIONS WHEN I GOT HOME. But the whole time I was separating eggs and slicing kiwi fruit and making sure everything was ready for my guests, that conversation with Kai was replaying in my head.

Could someone who seemed so cut-up about his girl-friend's death have killed her? On the other hand, had he really cared about Sam that much if he was seeing someone else at the same time? He was strong and known to have a volatile temper—he could easily have lost control. All it would take was a moment of madness.

But would he have told me she'd threatened to get him fired if he was guilty? Because it certainly gave him a motive, as well as a compelling reason to have lost his temper and killed her in the heat of the moment.

Nor did it explain the whole weird business with the car and the joyriding teenagers, or Sam telling her boss she was too sick to come to work and then heading off for some mysterious destination instead.

I shook my head. It just wasn't adding up—but I had a party to host. I determined to stop thinking about it for a while and enjoy the night with my friends instead. At a quarter to seven, everything in my place was ready for dessert, and I smoothed down the green dress I was wearing and hurried next door to Jack's.

At seven o'clock precisely, there was a knock on Jack's front door. Sherlock, who'd been washing himself on the lounge, leapt down and stalked upstairs. Apparently Jack's cat didn't approve of visitors.

Jack grinned at me. "Show time!"

It was Andrea and Nick and I introduced Andrea as Jack ushered them through the house to the new back deck.

"I got that book you recommended," Nick whispered as his lips brushed my cheek. "I'm going to give it to her after training on Tuesday. I hope she likes it."

"She'll love it," I said. Tuesday was Andrea's birthday. "Are you going to lunch together?"

"Just a coffee," he said in a wistful tone. I got the distinct impression he would have loved to take her to lunch and make a fuss of her special day. "I think she's having lunch with her sister."

A few more people arrived, some of Jack's nursing friends from the hospital. I let them in and got them sorted with drinks.

"I hear you're a reader," Andrea was saying to Jack when I came back. "Are you going to join the library? We have a huge range of books for a town this size. Lots of voracious readers here."

"I wouldn't say I was voracious," Jack said, "but I've been meaning to reread Dickens for ages."

Andrea's eyes lit up like stars. "Dickens!" She tucked her arm into his and steered him towards the table where we'd laid out cheese platters and other snacks. "Tell me more. Which one is your favourite?"

Nick's eyes followed them, a guarded quality to his gaze.

"Don't worry," I said to him. "He's way too young to tempt her. She's just excited to meet a fellow lover of the classics."

"Never could stand Dickens," he said, still gazing after them. "We had to read *David Copperfield* in high school and it nearly killed me. Most boring book on the planet."

"I haven't read that one, but I'm not a big Dickens fan. Not really a classics fan at all, with a few exceptions. I prefer fantasy and science fiction."

"Then why are you in a book club that only reads classics?"

"Aunt Evie. She's a force of nature." Aunt Evie appeared in the doorway at that moment, carrying a beautiful maidenhair fern. She'd let herself in. "Come on, I'll introduce you."

"This is for Jack," she said, after I kissed her on the cheek and introduced her to Nick. "I've got one for you, too, as a housewarming gift. I left it on your front step."

"Thank you! But we said no presents. Here, let me take that for you; it looks heavy."

"I'm seventy-two, darling, not ninety-two. I can hold a

pot plant without collapsing. Where is your new neighbour?"

I led her through the crowd to where Jack was talking to one of his friends from the hospital and her husband.

"Jack, this is my Aunt Evie. She has a present for you."

"That's so kind!" He kissed Aunt Evie on the cheek as he accepted the fern from her. Then he glanced at me. "Didn't we say no gifts?"

"Jack, one of the benefits of getting old is that you can ignore what other people tell you to do. Everyone should have at least one housewarming gift when they move into a new home. Rose, I didn't realise that was you—how are you?"

She started chatting to Jack's friend from the hospital, who was a middle-aged woman with a round, friendly face. She was as petite as Aunt Evie, but her husband was so tall and skinny he looked as though he'd been put on a rack and stretched.

Sarah and Emily from our book club arrived together. Sarah was blond, tanned, and at least a head taller than dainty, dark-haired Emily. She looked like a Viking towering over a delicate Chinese princess.

"Where's Troy?" I asked as I greeted them, referring to Sarah's husband.

"He's got a work Christmas party tonight," Sarah said.

"You didn't want to go?"

"Are you kidding? A dinner with a bunch of scientists and academics? They'll spend all night discussing research full of scientific names I can't even pronounce."

"Sounds like a yawn fest," Emily said, her glossy black hair swinging as she laughed.

"I was so thrilled when you invited us," Sarah said to me. "It gave me an excuse not to go!"

A couple more of Jack's friends arrived, two girls and a guy, all nurses. These ones were younger than Rose and her husband, about our own age.

"So this is the new deck, mate?" the guy asked.

We'd set up chairs around the edges against the railing. Jack had an outdoor table that would seat six comfortably, or eight at a pinch, which he'd pushed up against the back wall of the house to leave plenty of room for people to mingle. That was where we'd laid out the snacks and a do-it-yourself bar. The barbecue was next to it. Even with a dozen people here, there was still plenty of room.

Jack surveyed the deck proudly. "It turned out great, didn't it? All thanks to my mate Nick, here."

"So this is why you skipped the gym yesterday?" Andrea ran a hand over the sleek metal railing.

"Had to get it finished for the party," Nick said.

"You built it yourself?" one of the nurses asked. "It must have taken you ages."

"He only started on Monday," Jack said, beaming like a proud parent. "He's very talented."

"So it seems," Andrea said. "It looks wonderful, Nick."

"My Andy was very handy," Aunt Evie said. "You can't go wrong with a man who's good with his hands, I always say." She slanted a meaningful look at Andrea, who merely looked thoughtful.

One of the new arrivals had brought Jack a present, too, which turned out to be an apron with *kiss the cook* printed on it, which he immediately put on. "Time to fire up the barbie!"

Heidi and Dave arrived, also bearing gifts—a selection of teas for me and a bottle of wine for Jack.

"I brought some champagne, too," Heidi said as she hugged me, enveloping me in her soft floral scent. Her hugs weren't the half-hearted affairs of most social greetings, but full, crushing expressions of her affection. I hugged her back, even as I told her off for bringing presents when she wasn't supposed to. "It's just a bit of tea and champagne. Is this a party or not? You can't have a party without champagne."

"I'm sure Priya would approve," I said. Priya was always trying to add champagne to our book club meetings.

"Is she here?"

"She's running late. She texted me and said something had come up and not to wait for her."

The noise level rose as the delicious smell of sausages cooking started to drift from the barbecue. The men clustered around Jack at the barbecue while the women tended to clump together near the food table. I darted in and out of Jack's kitchen, tossing salads and bringing plates and cutlery to the table.

"Need a hand?" Heidi asked, sticking her head into the kitchen.

"Can you get the bread rolls out of the oven?" I was

hunting through Jack's cupboards for a bowl to put them in.

"Sure." She grabbed a set of oven mitts and got to work. "Is everyone here now?"

"I think so—apart from Priya, of course. Unless Jack has a couple more friends coming."

"Jack doesn't," the man himself said, ducking into the kitchen. He rummaged in the cutlery drawer until he came up triumphant with a bottle opener. "Everyone else is working tonight. The perils of having friends who do shift work."

"No Curtis tonight?" Heidi asked once he'd left again.

"He's working," I said, keeping my back to her. Part of me was busting to tell her every last detail of our exchange on the beach. That part was still thrilling at the warmth in his eyes when he'd looked at me, and how much he'd seemed to regret missing the party. The other part of me was aware that grown-ups had boundaries and only teenagers blabbed every detail of their love lives to their best friends. But my inner teen was winning the fight. Before she could spill her guts, I cast around desperately for something to say that wasn't, *Guess what? CURTIS HELD MY HAND.* "We were chatting earlier and he tried to apologise for Kelly being mean to me."

"Really? That's so sweet."

I know, right? And did I mention he held my hand?

"What's sweet?" That was Aunt Evie, wandering in looking for another drink. "What have I missed?"

"Charlie had a run-in with Kelly Parmenter on the beach," Heidi said.

"It wasn't a run-in," I said weakly, but Aunt Evie was already demanding to know what had happened, so I filled her in. Curtis's hands didn't get mentioned at all. I was quite proud of myself.

"There's a rumour going around the Lodge that she's taking drugs again," Aunt Evie said.

I blinked. "Really? Why on earth are they talking about her at the Lodge?"

"She's a very successful model, you know," Aunt Evie said. "Half the town hates her—"

"More than half," Heidi butted in.

"But everyone's interested in her," Aunt Evie finished. "She has such a glamorous life, always jetting off to some exotic location or other. She's the closest we've got to a local celebrity. Local girl made good—or bad, I suppose, if you take the drug thing into consideration."

"And you really have to take it into consideration when you're married to a policeman," Heidi said. "That was part of the reason their marriage fell apart."

"What was the other part?" I shouldn't ask, but I couldn't resist.

"Probably her personality," Aunt Evie said. "Awful woman. I can't think what a nice boy like Curtis ever saw in her. Where is he tonight, anyway?"

"At work," I said. "Why does everyone think Kelly is using? She looked fine when I saw her."

"She was probably wearing makeup," Aunt Evie said. "If you saw her without it you'd be shocked. Her skin's broken out, she's got circles blacker than the Ace of Spades under her eyes, and she's a terrible colour."

"When did *you* see her without makeup?"

"Oh, it wasn't me. But Cheryl has a friend who knows her cleaning lady, and *she* said that Kelly looked so bad she went and looked in her old hiding spot to see if there were any drugs there."

I had no idea who this Cheryl was, but I didn't doubt the story. The gossip grapevine was alive and well in Sunny Bay, and it was rarely wrong.

"And were there?" Heidi asked, as spellbound as I was.

"No, but that doesn't prove anything. What did you think of her, Charlie?"

"She's not very friendly, is she?"

Aunt Evie laughed. "She's one of those people who only bother being charming if they think they can get something out of you. And of course she's jealous of you."

"Of *me*? *She's* the supermodel! What's she got to be jealous about? She doesn't even know me."

"I'm sure Maisie has told her enough for her to realise that Curtis is interested in you."

I whirled around and pretended to dig around in a cupboard for something, certain that they would be able to guess my secret just by looking at my face. Yes, Curtis *was* interested. He'd said so only a few hours ago on the beach. "But they're divorced," I said to Jack's crockery. "Why should she care? Even if it were true."

"Oh, pish-tush." Aunt Evie waved her hand dismissively. "Of course it is."

"And she's jealous because she doesn't want anyone else succeeding where she failed," Heidi said.

Aunt Evie nodded. "Jealousy is as old as time. It's been

around since the first caveman fancied a rock that belonged to someone else and bashed him over the head and stole it."

"Besides," Heidi said. "She's probably afraid you'll make him happy, and she's so vindictive she couldn't bear for him to be happy. She's bound to hate you on sight."

"Great," I said. "That makes me feel so much better."

CHAPTER 17

AN HOUR LATER, WE MOVED NEXT DOOR FOR DESSERT. I HAD two large pavlovas and a big bowl of fruit salad ready to go. I'd also bought a couple of tubs of French vanilla ice cream, and there was soon a contented silence in my little lounge/dining room as people hoed into the food.

"This is really good pavlova," Sarah said around a mouthful of it.

"I know, right?" Heidi said. "Mine always cracks and falls apart, but this is perfect. Just the right amount of cream on top, too."

"You've got to let it cool down super slowly," said Rose, Jack's nurse friend. "I leave mine in the oven with the door ajar until it's stone cold."

"I think pavlova is my favourite dessert," Emily said. "I'd eat it every night if I could."

"Shame you didn't win the Powerball," Jack said. "You could have hired a personal chef to cook it for you."

Rose laughed. "Seven million would get you a lot of pavlova."

"I can't believe no one knows who the winner is," Sarah said. "That's a big secret to keep."

"But nobody knows the secret except the winner," I pointed out. "The newsagent doesn't know the identity of the person—they only know they sold the winning ticket."

"Right," Jack said. "And if they asked for their name not to be published, they obviously don't want anyone knowing, so they'll keep the secret."

"Secrets that big have a way of coming out," Aunt Evie said. "Trying to keep quiet about such a life-changing event is against human nature."

Jack got up to refill her wine glass. "Have you heard something?"

Smart man. He'd only known her for a couple of hours, and already he knew she was the one to turn to if you were looking for town gossip.

"Thank you, dear boy." She took a sip from her glass and smiled up at him. "No, I haven't, but I'm sure it will come out eventually. The winner will slip up, or they'll buy something they shouldn't have been able to afford, and people will figure it out."

"What would you buy, if you were the winner?" he asked her.

"Ha! You'd know I'd won straight away, because I'd be driving a brand-new sports car around town and wearing an enormous diamond on my finger."

"I'd go to Europe," Andrea said, "and see all the places I've only read about."

"I'd like to see Europe," Nick said. She smiled at him and raised her glass in his direction.

"I'd start a children's charity," Heidi said.

"Oh, now you're just making us look bad," Aunt Evie said, making me laugh.

"But surely you'd spend a bit of money on yourself," I said. "Seven million dollars is a lot of money. I'm sure the charity could spare some for you to treat yourself."

"Or even to treat me," her husband Dave suggested.

She laughed and licked cream off her spoon. "I might get a bigger house, I suppose. A big backyard for the boys to run around in would be lovely."

"Forget a house," Sarah said. "I'd buy an absolute *mansion*."

That made sense. Sarah and Troy were currently living with her parents because the builder who'd been building their dream home had been a crook. He'd taken their money but they still had no house, just a big fat legal headache.

Buying a house would probably be at the top of Jess's list, too, if she ever won the lottery, since she'd been fleeced by the very same builder. There were a dozen young couples in the area in the same boat. Although perhaps now Jess would inherit Sam's house.

"Mansions are all very well," Aunt Evie said, "but think of the cleaning!"

"I'd get a cleaner, too," Sarah said. "What about you, Charlie? What would you do with seven million dollars?"

I shrugged. "I don't know. I'm pretty happy with my

life at the moment. Maybe I'd take you all on a holiday with me."

"I'm in," Jack said. "Where are we going?"

"Europe," Andrea said immediately.

I grinned. "Apparently we're going to Europe, but I guess if we've got seven million to spend we can afford to squeeze in a few other destinations. Where would you like to go?"

"How about America? I've always wanted to see New York."

"And the Grand Canyon!" Rose said.

"Disneyland," Heidi added dreamily.

"You'd look cute in a pair of mouse ears," Emily said.

"Vegas for me," Aunt Evie said.

"You've just won seven million dollars," I protested. "You don't need Vegas!"

"No, *you've* won seven million dollars." She waved her wine glass at me, sloshing a little on the tablecloth. "I have to make my own fortune."

"I don't think Vegas is the right place for that," Rose said. "The only people who win there are the casino owners."

"Well, maybe I'll get rip-roaring drunk and get married to a complete stranger by an Elvis impersonator," Aunt Evie said.

"Whoa!" Jack held up both hands. "Okay, we're not letting you out of our sight when we get to Vegas."

I shook my head. "I think Vegas is officially off the itinerary."

"What if *you* won?" Rose asked Jack. "What would you

do with the money? I bet you wouldn't still be working night shift at Sunny Bay Community Hospital."

"I'd buy an Aston Martin."

Nick sat up straighter. "Oh, now we're talking."

Aunt Evie frowned. "One of those old-fashioned cars that Roger Moore drives in the James Bond movies?"

Jack laughed. "No, they have newer models now. Sexiest things you've ever seen. They cost a cool half million each."

"Actually, you know who has a new Jeep?" Nick said thoughtfully. "Kai Nguyen."

I glanced at Aunt Evie. We were probably all thinking the same thing. *They'll buy something they shouldn't have been able to afford.* "But it takes a while for a new car to come in after you order it. Longer than a couple of weeks."

Surely Kai couldn't have won the lottery *and* killed his girlfriend all in the same week? That was a mighty big week he was having, if so. Did being the big winner make him more or less likely to be the murderer? The whole thing seemed preposterous.

"Not necessarily," Nick said. "He could have walked into the dealership and bought one off the floor with cash. Maybe he's our winner."

"Didn't they just arrest him for killing that poor woman?" Rose asked.

"No, he got arrested for attacking a policeman," Andrea said. Gym gossip travelled fast. "But they let him off with a warning."

"But isn't he the only suspect?" Rose persisted. "I heard he was violent."

"He's not having a great week, let's put it that way," Andrea said. "It certainly looks bad for him, but I think the investigation is still only in its early stages."

"If he's won the lottery, *something's* going his way," Nick pointed out.

"Would the lotteries office have paid over the money that fast?" Jack asked.

"Don't see why not," Nick said. "They've got the cash just sitting there. All you have to do is give them your bank account details."

"How do you know?" Sarah asked, tossing her blond hair out of her face. "Have you ever won anything?"

"Stands to reason, doesn't it?"

"Are you sure *you're* not our big winner?" Andrea purred, fluttering her eyelashes theatrically. "Take me to Europe?"

He laughed. "If I was the winner, we'd be on the plane already."

The doorbell rang. "That'll be Priya," I said, and went to answer it.

"Finally!" Heidi said, when I brought her in a moment later. "You're lucky there's any pavlova left."

"As long as there's alcohol left," she said, flopping into my vacated chair. "Is that champagne? Thank God."

Jack jumped up. "Let me get you some."

"My saviour!"

"Priya, this is Jack," I said. "Jack, Priya."

"Hi." He gave her a big smile.

She took the champagne from him. "You are my new favourite person. Thanks."

And then she downed the whole thing in one go.

Jack's eyes widened. "Another?"

"Yes, please." She sipped at this one more slowly. "Did you guys hear the big news?"

"They found out who won the Powerball?" I asked.

"Bigger." She looked around at the circle of faces, making sure that every eye was on her. "Jess has been taken in for questioning again."

The way she said it, as if this was a major development, filled me with sudden dread. "Why?"

"Some new information. The time of death suggests that Sam was already dead at the time Annette saw her. They think she died some time early on Friday morning, between five and seven."

Nick frowned. "So they think Annette was lying?"

"What's that got to do with Jess?" Andrea asked at the same time.

Priya shook her head, eyes gleaming with excitement. "No, they don't think Annette was lying. They think she saw someone who looks exactly like Sam, leaving the house after Sam was dead."

She paused meaningfully to let that sink in. My heart sank. What possible reason could Jess have to leave Sam's house and get into her car and drive away, leaving her dead sister behind?

How could Jess be the killer? I'd been with her when she found her sister's body. I'd watched her fall to pieces, shattered by grief and shock, when moments before she'd been chatting happily to me. No one could be that good an actress.

"But what about Sam's text to Henry?" I asked. "That was sent around eight in the morning."

Priya gave me an impatient look. "It's easy enough to send a text on someone else's phone. Jess must have sent it after she killed her so that no one would raise the alarm when Sam didn't turn up for work that day."

"And then she hid the body under the bed and drove her car away as if she had gone to work?" Aunt Evie asked.

"But why do that if she'd already made the excuse that Sam wasn't going to work?" I asked. "That doesn't make sense. And Annette said she wasn't dressed in work clothes."

"Probably just to confuse the issue," Priya said. "To stop people looking for her too soon. To make it look as though Sam was still alive when she wasn't, so the police would be starting their investigation on the back foot. I bet she waited until she saw Annette in her front yard before she came outside and drove away."

I bit my lip, torn. *Someone who looks exactly like Sam.* I had a sudden memory of Jess sitting on Sam's couch, looking down at her hands as she told me they'd had a disagreement recently. But I couldn't believe she'd go that far. Not when I'd held her in my arms as she sobbed. Her grief had been so real. What kind of disagreement would be enough to make her kill her own twin?

"So maybe it was some other blond woman."

"Who just happened to look exactly like Sam?" Priya sounded doubtful.

"How sure are we that she did? If Annette only glanced at her, someone who only looked *similar* might have been enough to persuade her she was looking at Sam." I'd made the same mistake when I'd first seen the photo of Sam and Lauren at the lighthouse, after all. From across the room, I'd assumed it was a photo of the twins, simply because I could see two blond girls. Not until I got closer and saw how different they were did I realise my mistake.

"Some random blonde wouldn't have known who Sam's boss was, to send that text," Priya pointed out.

It was just as well Lauren had been at that conference when Sam was murdered, otherwise Priya would be suspecting *her* next.

"I'm sure the police will sort it out," Aunt Evie said.

"Also," Priya said, thoroughly enjoying her role as harbinger of doom, "apparently Sam always called Henry *Hens*, but the text said 'hi, Henry'. Henry mentioned it in his interview with the police, just as a throwaway comment, but that was what started them thinking that someone other than Sam may have sent the text. And then the new time of death was confirmed and it all fell into place."

"I can't believe this." I shook my head. "There must be some mistake. I just can't believe Jess would be capable of killing her own sister. She *loved* her."

Aunt Evie put a comforting hand on my arm. "Why don't you have another drink, darling? You look quite upset."

"Yes." Jack jumped up and grabbed a fresh bottle of champagne out of the cooler. "This is a night for celebrating. Let's toast new homes, new neighbours, and new friends."

He popped the cork and started pouring and passing glasses around.

"We should smash a bottle on the house," one of Jack's nurse friends said, a young guy who looked as though he'd drunk a few too many beers already.

"What on earth for?" Rose asked.

"They do it with ships," he said. "Launching a new ship, moving into a new house. Same thing. It's a celebration."

"Absolutely not," Priya said. She jumped up and took the bottle from Jack. "That would be a waste of champagne. Come with me."

"What are you doing?" I asked, but I followed her out the front door, along with a few of the others.

"Don't smash it," Jack said. "Cleaning up broken glass is no fun."

"I'm not going to smash it," she said, rolling her eyes at him. "This is good champagne."

She poured a little on the wall by my front steps, then leaned over the bushes that divided my driveway from Jack's and splashed a little on the bricks on his side, too.

"What exactly are you doing?" Jack asked, laughing.

"I'm ... launching ... your houses."

"They're not ships."

"Well, you're launching new lives in them, aren't you? That counts."

"That's right." Jack's drunk friend nodded enthusiastically. "Same thing."

Priya stood up straight and cleared her throat theatrically. "I hereby name these homes ... Party

Central." Then she took a long swallow from the bottle in her hand.

"Hey, leave some for the rest of us," Jack said.

"I've got some catching up to do," she said, but she offered him the bottle.

Holding her gaze, he drank from it, to cries of encouragement from the drunk friend, and laughter and protests from the rest of us. Priya watched him, a smug expression on her face.

I shook my head. "You guys are gross. We have perfectly good glasses inside."

Heidi laughed. "I thought nurses would have better hygiene standards."

"I'm not afraid of a few girl germs," Jack said.

"Well, don't drink it all." Priya took the bottle back and drank again, then put her arm through Jack's and dragged him back inside.

I got busy then, making coffee and tea for those who wanted it. Time flew by as I chatted with everyone. Jack's friends all seemed nice, even the drunk one, though he disgraced himself in the bushes by the front door on the way out. At least he hadn't thrown up in my house. Rose and her husband drove him home.

Aunt Evie left a few minutes later, saying she had an early start the next morning. "Lovely party, darling."

I was in the kitchen again, making myself another cup of tea, when Priya came in.

"Have you been having a good time?" I asked. She'd spent a long time chatting to Jack after the champagne incident. He'd even got her up dancing with a couple of his friends in my little courtyard.

"Sure. Great party." She smiled, but there was a forced note in her voice.

"You tired?" I asked. "Did you have to work tonight?"

"You mean because of the Jess thing? No."

"Oh." I'd thought it was a bit odd that she'd be working on a Saturday night, since the paper didn't come out on the weekends. "Why were you so late, then?"

She grimaced. "I had a family lunch that turned into a huge drama."

"Is everything all right?"

"Apart from the fact that I'm about to murder my mother, sure."

"Is this about the guy she wants you to meet?"

"Yeah." She slumped against the fridge and folded her arms across her chest. "That woman is the most stubborn person I know. She just wouldn't stop. And she's the queen of the guilt trip—she went on and on about the sacrifices she and Dad had made coming to this country so that we could have a better life, how hard they've worked for us, blah, blah, blah. I've heard it all before, but it makes me feel about this big." She held up her hand, thumb and first finger very close together.

"Why don't you just go and meet the guy?"

"Because then there'll be no stopping her. I gave in last time and she was immediately convinced we were getting married. There was so much pressure I had to move out. I'm sure I'd be married by now if I hadn't. It's so hard to say no to someone who simply won't accept that no is a possibility."

"That sounds pretty rough. But I'm sure she's only doing it because she loves you."

"I know, I know. That makes it worse. I hate to disappoint her, but it's my life. I'm not giving up my independence, even if it makes her miserable and we end up fighting all the time." She sighed and ran a hand through her hair. "In the end I only got out of there because I told her I had a boyfriend already."

I put my teacup down on the bench. "You what?"

"It was the only way to get out of meeting this guy. But then of course she was outraged that I hadn't told her before and how dare I go out with someone without introducing him to her." Her mouth twisted into a reluctant smile. "So now she's demanding I bring him to dinner next weekend to meet the family."

I stared at her, aghast. "But you don't have a boyfriend! What are you going to do?"

She shrugged. "I'll think of something."

CHAPTER 18

Sunday was a lazy day after the party the night before. Rufus had a particularly slow start—when I'd come back in after saying goodnight to the last guests, I'd found him slurping beer out of a glass someone had left on the floor by their chair. I grabbed the glass before he drank too much, but it obviously made him sleepy. We cuddled on the couch while I read *Middlemarch* for most of the afternoon. Our book club meeting was on Friday night and I was determined to finish it by then.

Mostly it seemed to be about the perils of marriage—or maybe I was reading it that way with Priya's dilemma so fresh in my mind. No one in the book seemed happy in their marriage, though they were all unhappy for different reasons. We definitely needed something different for our next book. *Frankenstein* was meant to be up next, but I wouldn't be surprised if Aunt Evie tried to weasel out of it again.

In between worrying about Priya, I worried about Jess,

just for a change of pace. Her issue was even more concerning. The evidence looked bad for her, there was no denying that. Kai must be happy that the heat was off him, at least. There was no way a muscular tattooed guy could be mistaken for Sam—if anyone was going to impersonate her after she was dead, her identical twin was the obvious choice.

Yet I still couldn't believe that Jess had done it. Sure, my track record for gullibility wasn't great—look how my faithless ex-fiancé had fooled me into thinking he was a stand-up guy, when all the time he'd been sleeping with my best friend. And she'd hoodwinked me, too. I'd thought we'd be friends for life.

When I'd first discovered how wrong I'd been about both of them, it had really shaken my self-confidence, and made me question everything and everyone. Was everyone showing me a false face? How could I ever trust my own judgement again? But as the weeks passed, I'd realised there'd been signs all along, which I'd explained away in order to keep the peace, when really I should have listened to my gut.

And right now, my gut was telling me that Jess was innocent.

On Monday morning, I picked up the photo of Sam I'd chosen from the printer. It was a large, portrait-sized print, and I bought a slim, elegant silver frame to put it in.

I hesitated on Jess's front doorstep. Maybe she wouldn't be here—perhaps she was at work. I chewed my lip, then raised my hand and knocked decisively. If there was no one home, I'd just leave it on the doorstep.

An older woman with curly black hair answered the door. This must be Jess's mother-in-law. "Yes?"

"Hi," I said, "I'm Charlie, the photographer—"

"If you're with the press you can get out of here." She scowled and started to shut the door.

"No, no," I said quickly. "I'm a friend of Jess's—I brought round a photo for the funeral."

She eyed the bag I was holding out as if it might contain a snake. "Wait here."

She closed the door, leaving me on the porch, and I heard her footsteps recede into the house. In a moment, a lighter, quicker tread approached and Jess herself opened the door.

"Come in," she said, her gaze darting around nervously. The minute I was inside she shut the door. "I'm sorry about that, we've had some trouble with the press. Gabriela is just trying to protect me."

"I understand. I just wanted to drop off the photo."

"She's been particularly on edge since the break-in." She led me into a bright, airy kitchen and gestured for me to take a seat at a round wooden table. "On top of the murder, it's been hard to take."

"You had a break-in? When was this?"

"On Friday night."

"How awful! Did they take much?"

"As far as we can tell, they didn't take anything at all. The police think they must have been disturbed. They made a terrible mess, though."

The table was set into a bay window that looked out over a neatly mown lawn bordered by roses. I folded my hands on the checked tablecloth. "I wasn't sure if you'd be at work."

"I haven't been going to work. Tea?" I nodded and she turned the kettle on and got two mugs out of a cupboard. "I just ... everything is so up in the air. I can't sleep. I can't think about anything else. And now the police are saying that couldn't have been her that Annette saw driving away. Nothing makes any sense." She stared out the window for a long moment while the kettle shrilled right in front of her. Then she switched it off and poured water into the mugs with a hand that shook. "I keep wanting to wake up, but the nightmare won't stop."

"I'm sorry. This must be so hard."

She handed me my tea and slipped into the seat across from me. She hadn't asked how I took it, so I just drank it black. She didn't touch her own, and I wondered how many cups of tea and been made and left untouched in the last few days. Tea was a wonderful comfort, but there were some situations that were beyond its powers.

She picked restlessly at the placemat in front of her. "Leo says we have to get a lawyer before I talk to the police again. I know it looks bad, but how can they think I'd kill my own sister?"

I put my hand over hers, stilling her restless fingers. "*I* don't think you killed her."

She turned her hand to squeeze mine, then released it. "Thank you. That means a lot. Henry rang earlier, too, to express his support."

"Henry?" I had a blank moment. "Oh, Sam's boss?"

She nodded. "He blames himself. He was at an

accounting conference in the Hunter on the day she died. Sam didn't want to attend this year. He thinks if he'd made her go, she'd still be alive."

That was tough. "Lauren was at a conference in the Hunter, too. I wonder if it was the same one?"

"It was. He said he saw her there. He knows her a little through Sam. They were both in one of the morning sessions together on the day Sam ... on the day she ..." She cleared her throat. "Well. Sam would have had fun with both of them there. I can't help wishing he'd tried a little harder to persuade her."

I felt so sad for her. She looked so forlorn. "I'm sorry. I hope they find who did it soon."

"You'd be surprised how many people think *I* did it." Her voice shook.

"They're idiots, then," I said. "Ignore them."

"I can't ignore the police." She clutched her mug, wrapping her fingers around it to warm them. "They're not saying it yet, but I can tell they think I did it."

I sipped my tea cautiously. It was hot without milk. "I'm guessing you don't have an alibi?"

"No. I don't work on Fridays, and I left the house early." She leaned in and lowered her voice. "Gabriela does her best, but living with your mother-in-law is hard. I usually get out of the house as soon as I can on my days off and spend the day somewhere else. It was a lovely day, so I decided to do the trail from Sunny Bay around to Long Reef."

"A hiking trail?"

"Yeah. It's a four-hour hike. I left home about six-thirty. I was meeting a friend for lunch, and I wanted to do the hike and get back here in time to shower and change before lunch."

"Did anyone see you that morning?"

She shrugged. "I said goodbye to Leo before he left for work. I passed a couple of joggers on the trail, but no one I knew."

She looked at me with big, troubled eyes. That meant no one could ID her and prove that she was on the hiking trail when she said she was. And I doubted the police would take her husband's word that he'd seen her at six-thirty. Of course he would lie to protect his wife.

And maybe, they'd think, she *had* hit the trail ... after she'd killed her sister and paraded herself in front of the neighbour. I wondered how close the trail head was to the skate park where Sam's car had been found. Knowing Jess's luck, it would probably be close—everything was pretty close in a small place like Sunny Bay.

"Was your mother-in-law here when you got home?"

"Yes, but that was almost midday. They say Sam died sometime between five and seven in the morning. Blunt force trauma." She looked away for a moment, fighting for control. When she looked back at me, her expression was fierce. "And you know what's the worst part?"

"What?"

"That while the police are convincing themselves that *I* did it, they're not even looking for the real killer anymore." She clenched her fists. "I can't stand knowing that man is walking around out there, totally in the clear."

"Which man? Kai?"

"Can there be any doubt? Of course he killed her—and now he's going to get away with it."

"But ..." I'd thought Kai was probably the killer, too, but this latest evidence messed with the neat little case the police had been building against him. "But if it was Kai, how do you explain the blond woman that Annette saw? If Sam was already dead by then, who was it?"

She shrugged. "They're probably wrong about the time of death. How can they be so sure, when we didn't find her until Monday? Or if they're right, Annette is lying."

"But why would she lie?" Sam's next door neighbour had nothing to gain from confusing the investigation with made-up evidence.

Jess crossed her arms and stared at me with defiance. "Well, maybe she's not lying. Maybe she's just getting her days mixed up, and she's remembering seeing Sam go to work on some other day."

"Maybe." That didn't seem terribly likely to me either, but there was no point arguing with Jess about it. It certainly wouldn't help her current situation. But perhaps it would be worth having another chat with Annette, just in case Jess was right. That would take a whole lot of heat off her. I picked up the bag I'd brought with me and pulled out the photo of Sam. "I'm sure the facts will come out in the end. In the meantime, I brought this for you."

She took it from me almost reverently and gazed at it for a long time in silence, her eyes welling with tears. "It's beautiful." She looked up at me and attempted a smile. "We had a lot of fun that day, didn't we?"

"We did." The two of them had been laughing and joking around, though Jess had seemed more at ease than her sister. Sam had been a little withdrawn at first, but she'd warmed up after a while. "It was one of my favourite photo shoots. And you both looked so cute in your matching caps."

"And the T-shirts," Jess said, still gazing fondly at the photo. "She complained so much about wearing matching outfits, you'd think I'd asked her to wear chain mail. She was like that as a kid, too—at least, after she and Lauren got so chummy. But Mum just ignored her."

"How are your Mum and Dad coping?"

She looked up, her gaze bleak. "Not well. I think we'll all feel better after the funeral. We're just kind of stuck in limbo now."

"When is the funeral?"

"The coroner is releasing the body to us on Thursday, so it will be next week some time, probably Tuesday. Then my brother and his family will fly back to Perth."

"And your parents? You said they live in Melbourne?"

"They're going to stay a bit longer, in case ... in case I need them." She looked down at the photo again. "Would you ... would you come to the funeral?

"Of course," I said, surprised. "If you'd like me to."

"We're keeping it to family and friends. Funerals are never easy, are they? But this one is going to be tough. I'm frightened the press will be hanging around, and there are bound to be gawkers, too, especially now that the police have ... well, especially now. Everyone wants to stare at the girl who killed her twin sister." She shook her head. "Even some of Sam's friends think that ... think that I ..."

That she was the killer. My heart broke for her. As if it wasn't bad enough to lose your sister in such a horrible way, without having people accusing you of killing her.

"I'm sure no one who knows you would believe that," I said.

"Maybe. But it would be nice to see a friendly face there."

"I'll be there," I promised. "You can count on me."

CHAPTER 19

IT RAINED FOR THE NEXT COUPLE OF DAYS, BUT IT WAS STILL hot, so the air felt thick and unpleasantly muggy. Even the usual sea breeze failed us, and Sunny Bay sweltered. I stayed inside for the most part, reading and uploading photos to my website, though I had one photo shoot booked for an engaged couple. We'd meant to shoot on the beach but, given the weather, we stayed indoors. At least the grey light was good for portraits, and I got some nice shots of the happy couple against rain-spattered windows, and on the porch swing of her parents' house.

Rufus didn't enjoy the heat at all. He flopped around the house and sighed heavily whenever I moved to a different room, since he seemed to feel compelled to follow me wherever I went. Just in case a crazed killer should jump out from behind the curtains, I supposed. He also cast many meaningful glances at the front door. Even though I showed him the rain through the windows and told him it was too wet to go for a walk, he wasn't convinced.

Thursday dawned bright and clear. It was even a bit cooler, with a sea breeze blowing the sticky heat away. I didn't know which of us was more relieved to get out of the house. Even though I'd spent years in an office job, I'd quickly become used to my more flexible working life as a photographer, and I liked being able to get outside during the day. Rufus, of course, had spent the last couple of years living with Mrs Johnson next door, and she had pretty much given him the run of Sunny Bay, letting him out the front door in the morning and leaving it to him to return when he felt like it.

"Let's go, boy," I said after breakfast, and his ears pricked up. He bounded to the front door and stood looking back impatiently at me, his tail wagging furiously. "Oh, you want to go, do you? You want to go for a walk?"

The W word worked its usual magic. He barked and spun in a tight, crazy circle.

I laughed. "Okay, okay, I'm coming. Where shall we go?"

I opened the door and he was off like a bullet from a gun, only slowing his mad rush when he came to the first telegraph pole, which had to be sniffed with exquisite care before he lifted his leg to leave his calling card. I strode along behind him, letting him go wherever he wished, expecting him to head for the beach.

In fact, he turned at the surf club and headed down towards Sam's street. Perhaps he remembered Lauren's dog and was looking for a friend. I was happy to fall in with his wishes, since I'd meant to talk to Annette again if I could.

The police tape was gone from Sam's house, but there was no sign of Annette. Maybe she figured her garden had had enough water with all the rain. I continued on past her house, following the waving flag of Rufus's tail.

I mean, I could have knocked, but that would have felt a bit awkward. What would I say? *I've come to ask if you were lying to the police* wouldn't go down well. I'd really prefer to just sneak my questions into an innocent conversation. So we continued with our walk while I mulled over possible excuses for knocking on Annette's door.

Rufus would have led me all the way to Waterloo Bay, I was sure. He was still trotting along with as much energy as when we started, but I was starting to flag. Eventually I stopped him in a small reserve and sat down on a park bench to enjoy how fresh and green the world looked after the rain. After a quick circuit of the reserve, he threw himself down at my feet, panting.

It was nearly two hours later by the time we approached Annette's house again and I was no closer to a believable excuse for disturbing her. Fortunately for me, no excuse was necessary, since she was sitting on her front porch with her feet up, soaking in the sunlight. She was wearing glasses and holding one hand up to cover her right eye. As I watched, she swapped hands and covered her left eye instead.

"Hello," I called, stopping at the front gate. She swapped hands again and frowned. "Are you okay? Is something wrong with your eyes?"

She squinted in my direction, then got up and ambled down the path towards me. "Cataract surgery. They've just done the first eye. I've got to go back and get the other one done next month."

"Oh! I didn't know you had cataracts."

"Well, it's not as though you can see them, can you?" She sounded a little impatient. "They told me things would look bluer. I keep looking at everything with one eye and then the other. I can't believe the difference."

"Are your cataracts very bad?"

"Bad enough to operate. I'm hoping my sight will be much better after this. It would want to be—the operation costs enough."

"So you've had bad eyesight for a while?" I asked. Strange, I'd never seen her wearing glasses before. "Do you wear contacts?"

"Nope. Can't stand the things. I only used to wear the glasses for driving and watching TV. I can see well enough to get around the house without them. But they told me I have to wear them all the time now until I get my other eye done." She pointed at her right eye. "They put plain glass in this side. Everything still looks a bit blurry but they said my vision should clear soon. It's already better than it was before."

"Were you wearing glasses the day Sam died? When you saw her get into her car and drive away?"

She gave me a sharp look. "I don't know. Probably not. I was only watering the garden."

I wondered if the police knew that their witness was half-blind with cataracts. Maybe Annette hadn't been lying or confused about the day at all. Maybe she'd just seen a random blond woman and assumed it was Sam. I mean, that could be possible even for someone without sight issues, couldn't it? People saw what they expected to see. If you saw a woman come out of your neighbour's house and get into your neighbour's car, you would be fairly safe to assume that the woman was your neighbour. Especially if you only glanced that way for a moment. If you didn't want to meet her eyes because you didn't get along.

"Well, I just wondered ... maybe it wasn't Sam at all."

"Of course it wasn't."

I blinked. "But you told the police—"

"I told them it was her because that's how it seemed at the time. But now it's obvious it must have been that sister of hers, because she was already dead."

"You can't be sure of that."

She laughed in a rather sneering way. "Who else would it be? They're identical twins. I don't know why the police haven't arrested her already. It's obvious she killed her."

"It's not obvious to *me*. It could have been some other blond woman. Heaven knows there are enough of them in Sunny Bay." And very few of them were natural blondes, I was willing to bet.

"She was wearing that hat she always wore when she went jogging. The bright pink one."

Yes, the pink cap with the sparkly *Princess* on it. I didn't see how that proved anything. If the woman had just come out of Sam's house, she obviously had access to Sam's wardrobe. That still didn't prove it had to be Jess.

Although Jess did have one of those caps herself.

No, I told myself firmly. I am *not* going to start suspecting Jess.

"But she wasn't wearing running clothes, was she? You said before she was wearing jeans."

"I don't see what difference that makes. Those two were fighting, you know—or didn't you know that?"

I bit my lip. Jess had mentioned a *disagreement*, which didn't sound nearly as bad as a *fight*. Was Annette exaggerating?

"Oh, yes," she said, all smug now. "Heard them shouting at each other a while back there. Going at it hammer and tongs. That sister of hers used to be over here all the time, but not lately, no. Not since they had that big blow-up."

I frowned. I'd seen a little tension, maybe, at the photo shoot. As if they were easing back into being comfortable with each other. Jess had said the shoot was her way of apologising. Apologising for what? It seemed important to find out, if only so I could banish these lingering doubts about Jess.

"I just did a big photo shoot with them for their birthday. They were getting along just fine." Well, fine-*ish*. But Annette didn't need to know that. "Do you know what this supposed fight was about?"

She gave me an unfriendly look. "There was no supposed about it. That Jess went storming out, all upset. I tell you, this street is going to be a lot quieter without

Sam next door. She liked the drama, that's for sure. Always fighting with someone or other."

"But this particular fight," I prompted.

"No idea. I used to just turn the music up louder whenever she started up her screaming. This used to be such a quiet little street before she moved in."

I folded my arms and dug in. "Even supposing they did fight—they were twins. They were very close. Jess loved her sister."

"She's got *you* fooled, hasn't she? Never could stand either of them. We'll see who's right. I bet you any day now the police will be making an arrest, and I certainly won't be shedding any tears. Good riddance to the both of them."

And she marched up her pathway and disappeared inside.

CHAPTER 20

On Friday afternoon I took a stroll into town to the bottle shop. Our book club meeting was that evening and I thought I might take a bottle of champagne along. I'd been thinking about Priya's dilemma with her mother, which seemed an impossible situation, and I thought she might need some cheering up.

Rufus, of course, accompanied me, trotting along at my side or ranging out to investigate any promising smells. Lesser dogs—those who were trapped in their own yards or inside their houses—barked at him as he passed, but he treated them with the disdain they deserved, never acknowledging their unworthy presences. If he happened to mark a telegraph pole or a gate post right outside their house, well, that was pure coincidence, and not at all him flaunting his freedom to the world.

The man behind the counter of the bottle shop looked up as we entered. I always tried to get Rufus to wait outside when I went inside a store, but I wasn't always successful. He seemed convinced that some places were just too dangerous to let me enter by myself.

"I'll need to see some ID," the man said.

I blinked. At twenty-nine, I supposed it was flattering to be ID-checked, but it was a little perplexing, too. I knew I didn't look as though I was in my teens anymore. I couldn't remember the last time someone had asked for my ID.

"Really?" I asked. "Do I look that young?"

He was an older man with a neat moustache and dark eyes that twinkled as he grinned at me. The nametag on his shirt said *Dan*. "Not yours, love. His. He looks too young to be buying alcohol."

I smiled back. "He's three, which is twenty-one in dog years, so I think he's safe." I'd checked the pedigree papers after Nick had asked me how old Rufus was.

"Can't be too careful," he said. "Kids these days will try anything. Must think I came down in the last shower."

I grinned. "I don't think alcohol is really his thing, anyway. Although he did steal a few slurps of beer out of someone's glass on Saturday night. But I think he had a headache the next day, so hopefully he's learned his lesson." He'd certainly seemed slower than usual on Sunday.

"Can I help you with something, or are you happy to browse?"

"I'm looking for a nice champagne. Maybe a pink one."

He led me over to the champagne shelf. "This one's my

bestseller—very nice, a little sweeter than normal, and reasonably priced. Or if you prefer something drier, this one's very popular, too."

"Sweet is good," I said. I'd never cared for dry wines much. And judging by the champagne that Priya had brought to the last book club meeting, she felt the same.

The electronic bell over the door buzzed as two more people came in. Dan looked over and scowled. "School kids. Coming in here with their backpacks hoping to nick a bottle or two when I'm not looking." He raised his voice. "You can leave those packs outside, thanks very much—or even better, you can take yourselves off. You don't look old enough to shave, mate. You're certainly not old enough to buy anything in here."

"Just looking," the boy said in a surly tone, though he dumped his bag beside the door. "No law against that, is there?"

I realised I knew the girl with him, though she looked different in her school uniform. Younger. It was Annette's daughter, Grace. Something flashed in the sunlight as she heaved her bag off her shoulder and dumped it on the floor next to the boy's. I frowned, then came closer, the bottle of champagne still clutched in my hand.

"Where did you get that?" I asked. I put the bottle on the counter and bent to examine the charm swinging from the zipper on her bag. It was a J covered in diamantes. I gave the girl a sharp look.

Grace shrugged, her gaze sliding to the side. "I dunno. Some shop in Newcastle."

I didn't believe her for a minute. Some coincidences were too big to swallow. I bet if Jess were here right now, she'd identify this charm as belonging on her sister's keyring.

"Are you sure about that?" I watched her carefully, alert for any sign she was lying. "Which shop?"

"Don't remember." She flicked blond hair over her shoulder carelessly, but didn't meet my eyes.

I folded my arms across my chest and stared her down. "Why do you have a J on your bag when your name starts with G?"

"My boyfriend's name is Josh," she said. "Duh."

Rufus came out from behind a shelf of cabernets and her sullen expression was replaced with a smile. "Josh, look! There's a dog in the shop." Rufus trotted over to me and submitted to being patted by Grace. "He yours?"

"You want me to ring you up?" Dan asked. He was waiting behind the counter with my champagne in one hand and a brown paper bag in the other. "Or are you happy to browse for a while?"

"I'll just take the champagne," I said. From the corner of my eye I caught Grace jerking her head at the door, signalling to Josh that they should leave. She moved closer to her school bag, blocking my view of the charm. I became more and more certain that I was right.

I tapped my credit card on the terminal, then accepted the bottle in its brown paper bag. Then I turned my attention back to Grace, who had her bag back over her shoulder and was waiting impatiently in the doorway for Josh.

"So," I said. "Are you two the kids who stole Sam Middleton's car last week?"

Grace went perfectly still and the colour drained from her face. Josh shoved his thumbs through his belt loops and said, "It's not stealing if some idiot leaves the keys in the car."

"Josh," Grace hissed.

"What? She already knows. It's no big deal."

"Are you police?" Grace asked, sullen but without her boyfriend's bravado.

"Doesn't matter if she is," Josh said. "They can't do nothing. They don't send people to prison for a little joyride."

"Didn't you think it was odd that the keys were left in the car?" I asked. Could I believe them about that? Maybe they'd stolen it from Sam's place.

Maybe Grace was Annette's blonde.

No, that was ridiculous. Surely the woman couldn't be so blind that she couldn't recognise her own daughter?

But she said she only glanced at "Sam". And she was wearing that stupid pink cap. I eyed Grace's long blond hair. With her hair shoved up under a cap, she might look different enough that a quick glance could fool a woman with cataracts.

Suddenly I remembered how Annette had seemed in such a hurry to shoo Grace inside that first time I'd seen the girl. It had been so marked that I'd wondered at the time if she wanted to hide her daughter from me. Had Annette finally figured out it was her daughter she'd seen coming out of Sam's house? Maybe that was why she was trying so hard to throw suspicion on Jess.

Josh picked up his bag and slung it over his shoulder. "People do stupid stuff all the time."

"And whose idea was it to take the car for a ride? Yours?"

He shifted from foot to foot, impatient to be gone. "Nah."

"We don't know how to drive," Grace said. Now the game was up, she must have decided it was safer to be cooperative. "It was Callum's idea. He's seventeen."

"Was it his idea to set fire to it, too?"

"Why do you care?" Josh said. "You looking for Callum?"

"No. I'm just curious about that charm." I looked straight into Grace's eyes. "It doesn't belong to you."

"Come on, Josh, let's go," she said, reaching for his hand.

"You don't know nothing," he said to me fiercely, then he followed her out of the shop.

I breathed out a deep sigh.

"Problem?" Dan asked. "Have those little thieves snitched something of yours?"

"No."

"You seem upset. Are you okay?"

I took a firmer grip on my bottle of champagne. "I'm fine, thanks, Dan."

He smiled. "And what's your name, love?"

"Charlie."

"Well, you take care, Charlie. Hopefully I'll see you again soon."

I nodded and left the shop with Rufus shadowing my footsteps. I felt as though the answer to the mystery was just out of reach, which was immensely frustrating. Was I still missing a piece? I just couldn't make a sensible picture out of it.

Say that the three kids had stolen the car and that it had been Grace wearing Sam's cap that Annette had seen. Did that mean that they'd killed her? My heart said no. Grace was fifteen. What fifteen-year-old could murder a woman in cold blood, then help herself to the woman's wardrobe and drive away in her car?

Though, actually, Grace had just told me that she couldn't drive. Now, why had she been so keen to tell me that? Was she trying to mislead me?

Maybe the missing Callum was the killer, and Grace had been helping to cover it up by impersonating Sam. If they were friends, that might be possible, though given how jumpy she'd been in the bottle shop, when I'd only been asking about the charm, it was hard to believe she would be able to carry that off.

That still left the problem of Annette not recognising her own daughter. Which, okay, her eyesight wasn't the best, but that seemed improbable to me. If you'd lived with a person their whole life, you knew the way they walked, the way they stood—a simple baseball cap shouldn't be enough of a distraction.

But.

People saw what they expected to see. That was as

true now as it had been yesterday when I'd first thought it, talking to Annette herself.

"This whole thing is such a mess," I said to Rufus as we walked across the pedestrian crossing towards the newsagent.

The other option was that Annette had reported the sighting before she'd realised it was actually her own daughter and now she was lying to protect her. I supposed there was another possibility, too—Jess could be right, and Annette could be outright lying about having seen a woman leave the house at all. Maybe the whole "woman in a pink cap" thing was a story she'd invented. Though why she should do that I was having trouble imagining.

Maybe she was trying to confuse the police because she herself was the killer. I mean, if I'd gotten to the point where I was suspecting a fifteen-year-old kid, why not suspect her mother too? It made about as much sense as anything else. Annette could even be considered to have a motive, if a dispute about a tree could be taken that far. People had killed for less.

I looked up and saw the handmade sign still in the window of the newsagent. They were certainly proud of having sold the winning ticket. Would that sign still be there at Christmas? How long were they going to leave it up? It wasn't as though there had been any actual skill on their part—it was just the luck of the draw. It must be a good marketing tool.

They'd even added the winning numbers at the bottom of the sign, like parents proud of their three-year-old's drawing. I ran my eye over them, smiling. At least someone in Sunny Bay must be pretty happy. Was Nick right and it was Kai? We'd probably never know.

"Whoever it is, they're probably rolling in their cash and eating caviar right now," I said to Rufus. He wagged his tail but kept trotting along. He didn't give a hoot about the mysterious lottery winner—but he was probably the only one in town who didn't.

CHAPTER 21

"Would you know Brenda if you saw her in the distance?"
I asked Aunt Evie later. I'd bought some of her favourite
tarts from the little bakery in town—and some of mine—
and taken them round to her villa at Sunrise Lodge for
afternoon tea.

"What an odd question." She tipped her head to one
side, which set her giant earrings swinging. "You mean *my*
Brenda?"

"Yes. Your daughter Brenda. How many other Brendas
do you know? Wait, don't answer that." I didn't want to
derail the conversation completely. "Do you think you
would always know it was her, even if you only took a
quick glance?"

"Do I have my glasses on in this scenario?" She set a
cup of tea on the table in front of me and sat down
opposite.

That was a good point. "No, actually."

"Am I drunk?"

I smiled. Trust Aunt Evie to get into the spirit of things.

"You're not drunk, it's broad daylight, and she's thirty feet away, walking to her car. Would you know it was her?"

She hesitated. "I think so? When you live with someone for years, you know the way they move. You recognise their shape, even if you're not close enough to make out their face. But I suppose I might be distracted by something else." She took a bite of her Neenish tart and sighed in pleasure. "Or she might be wearing one of those inflatable dinosaur costumes. I wouldn't know it was her then."

I laughed. "She wouldn't be able to drive in an inflatable dinosaur costume."

"Do you think so?" She appeared to give it some thought, then shrugged. "I suppose you're right. But it would be funny, wouldn't it? Imagine if the police pulled her over. She could be arrested for driving while dinosaured."

I took a citrus tart for myself. Aunt Evie was welcome to all the Neenish tarts—I couldn't stand their gooey cream filling. "You say the strangest things sometimes."

"Darling, *I'm* not the one inventing odd scenarios and trying to work out if I would know my own daughter. What on earth is going on in that head of yours?"

I bit into my tart. The sharp tang of citrus and the buttery flakiness of the pastry combined to form an explosion of tasty goodness in my mouth.

"Just wondering about something," I said when I

could speak again. "I spoke to Annette yesterday. She's had a cataract operation."

"Really?"

I went on to fill Aunt Evie in on the conversation with Annette and my meeting with Grace in town earlier, and how I was sure the charm dangling from her backpack was Sam's.

"So now I'm wondering if the blond woman Annette saw could possibly have been her own child."

Aunt Evie's face screwed up in distress. "Yes, but surely you're not going to accuse a fifteen-year-old girl of murdering that poor woman? She's barely more than a child. How could she do such a monstrous thing?" And then, always practical, she added, "Sam would have been stronger than her anyway. How could she overpower her?"

"I'm sure it would be possible. All we know is that she died of a blow to the head." *Blunt force trauma* was what the police had told Jess and the family. "The killer could have sneaked up and hit her from behind. But anyway, I don't think Grace is the killer. But I do wonder if she's covering for someone else. There's another kid involved who already had a police record."

"Or perhaps she only stole the car and had nothing to do with the murder."

"That's certainly an option, too." I took a sip of tea to wash down the last of my tart. Such a strange topic to be discussing over a civilised afternoon tea. "I certainly hope the police are further ahead with their investigation than I am."

Aunt Evie sat up straighter and clasped her hands

together in pleasure. "Oh, I'm so glad you've taken the case on. You're so good at solving murders."

"You make me sound like a private detective," I protested. "I haven't *taken the case on* at all. Detective McGovern would have my hide if I got involved in another one of his investigations."

She gave me a shrewd look over the rim of her teacup. "I see. So you're not at all interested in the outcome of this case. You don't care who murdered poor Sam or what might happen to Jess now that she's the focus of the investigation."

"I didn't say that."

"You're not even intrigued by the mystery of the blond woman Annette saw," she went on inexorably. "That's why you've been sitting here stewing over it for the last ten minutes."

"I would just hate for Jess to end up suffering any more than she already has," I burst out. "McGovern is probably a stand-up guy, but he's keen to get a conviction."

"And you think he won't look at all the evidence properly?" she said, putting her cup down on its saucer. "I'm sure they teach them how to do that at detective school."

"It's a confusing case," I said huffily, not wanting to answer her question. It wasn't that I didn't trust McGovern exactly … I just felt compelled to fix this horrible mess for Jess.

"It certainly is. And if what Annette told you is true, and Sam and Jess were actually fighting before her death, it doesn't look good for Jess. I wonder what they were fighting about?"

"Probably nothing significant. Jess said it was just a sibling thing. Annette didn't like Sam, so she could be blowing some little tiff up into something much bigger."

"Uh-huh." Aunt Evie nodded, watching me with an indulgent smile. "It would probably be helpful to find out what that fight was about, wouldn't it?"

"Detective McGovern probably already knows," I said, but I wasn't convincing either of us. I didn't actually care what McGovern knew or didn't know. *I* wanted to know. And the way my aunt was smirking at me meant that she knew that, too.

"You should ask Jess," she said mildly, hiding her smile in her teacup.

"That would feel like accusing her," I said. Poor Jess had enough on her plate already without being cross-examined by someone outside the police force. She was probably sick of answering questions by now.

How else could I get the information? Annette said she hadn't heard what they were fighting about—perhaps Grace had? But I dismissed that idea as soon as it occurred to me. There wasn't much chance that Grace would help me after our little confrontation in the bottle shop. I'd practically accused her of murdering Sam.

"I wonder if Lauren knows?" I said to myself.

"The best friend? Quite possibly. Or even the boyfriend. Sam probably told at least one of them."

I shuddered at the thought of approaching Kai for help. Even with the police turning their attention to Jess now, he was still a suspect—he wouldn't take kindly to being prodded for information that might help strengthen the case against him. Lauren would be more likely to help me, since I'd found her dog for her.

"I might drop in on Lauren tomorrow morning," I said.

Aunt Evie smiled. "What a good idea." As if the whole thing hadn't been her idea to start with. "Now, how's that young man of yours?"

For a startled moment I thought she meant Will, then I realised she was talking about Curtis. I jumped up and grabbed her plate and mine and took them to her tiny kitchen. Why was I blushing just because I'd held his hand?

"I don't have a young man."

"You should. You should snap him up before someone else swoops in and takes him off the market."

"Aunt Evie!" I rinsed the plates, clattering around to hide my embarrassment. "You make him sound like a used car."

She laughed behind me. "Then hop in and take him for a ride, darling. What are you waiting for? The best way to get over a failed romance is to start a new one."

"It was a little more than just a romance."

"Nevertheless." She pushed me out of the way and started filling the sink with hot water and detergent. "Leave that, darling, I'll do it." Then she turned and fixed me with her best Serious Look. I'd seen that look plenty of times growing up, whenever Aunt Evie thought I could benefit from some of her hard-won wisdom.

"This business with Sam should have made it abundantly clear to you," she said sternly, "that none of us know how much time we have here. Life is not a dress rehearsal, sweetheart. Don't waste any more of your precious time on Will. You could be dead next week."

"Thanks."

"Well, it's true," she insisted. "And would you really want to go to your grave without kissing Curtis Kane at least once?"

"You are a terrible person," I said fondly as I dropped a kiss on her cheek. "I have to go."

She waved the washing-up brush sternly at me. "I'm only telling it like it is."

I grinned. "Love you."

"I love you, too. Don't forget what I said."

"I won't." I hesitated at the door. "Actually, there might be something happening there."

Her eyes lit up. "With Curtis?"

"Yes. But I don't want to jinx myself by talking about it too soon," I added as she opened her mouth, probably to fire a dozen questions at me. "See you tonight!"

I closed the door behind me and escaped before she could protest.

As it turned out, I didn't have to go and see Lauren the next morning; as I was walking along Beach Road on my way home, I spotted her on the sand throwing sticks for Benson. I took off my sandals and went down the steps to the beach, angling so that my path would intersect hers.

"Hi, Lauren. Benson all recovered from his adventure?"

"Oh, hi, Charlie. Yes, he's fine. He wasn't happy with me when I put chicken wire across the gap where he'd dug his hole, but he'll get over it."

"I have a digger, too," I said. "Rufus is a digging machine."

"He's not with you today?"

"No. We had our walk earlier." It was on the tip of my tongue to tell her about my meeting with Grace, but it wouldn't be fair to Grace to spread my theories around. I knew Aunt Evie wouldn't start any gossip, but I wasn't sure Lauren would feel the same restraint. Having seen how much Jess was suffering under mistaken accusations, it didn't seem right to subject a fifteen-year-old to the same ordeal. "I've just been visiting my aunt and I saw you down on the beach. There's something I wanted to talk to you about."

"Oh? What's that?"

Benson came charging back with his stick and dropped it at her feet. I smiled as I watched her throw it again for him. He wasn't even half Rufus's size, but he was very cute.

"I wondered if you knew whether Sam and Jess had been fighting before she died."

"Oh, yes. They were barely speaking for a few weeks there. They'd only started patching it up just before she died."

"Do you know what it was about?"

"Just Jess being Jess," she said bitterly. "She's older by three minutes, did you know that?"

I shook my head.

"I'm surprised she didn't manage to slip it into the conversation somewhere. In her mind, it's some big deal that makes her somehow better than Sam. She always expected Sam to do whatever she wanted her to. In high school, she thought she should have first choice out of Sam's wardrobe, even if Sam wanted to wear whatever it was herself."

"I thought they dressed identically when they were young?"

"That only lasted until Sam hit puberty. Then she put her foot down. And she always had better taste in clothes than Jess, so her wardrobe was better."

"Right. But lately, what did they fight about?"

"Same as always. Sam had something Jess wanted, so she thought Sam should just give it to her."

Benson galloped back towards us again with his stick, though he swerved to menace a couple of gulls who were resting on the beach. They took off, squawking angrily at him.

"And what was it?"

Lauren threw Benson's stick again, and it landed in the shallow water. The dog took off after it, his ears streaming behind him.

"Her house."

I blinked. "Jess was demanding that Sam give her her *house*?"

That was the most unreasonable thing I'd ever heard of, and sounded very unlike the Jess I knew.

"Not exactly. She wanted Sam to let her and Leo move in. She was sick of living with Leo's parents."

"And Sam didn't want her to?"

"Sam had ... a busy dating life. She liked having her own space, so she could bring anyone home whenever she wanted to, without having to deal with housemates. Having Jess and Leo there would have cramped her style."

"But Jess wasn't happy with that answer?"

"Jess isn't used to hearing the word *no* from anyone, least of all Sam. But Sam wasn't letting her sister walk all over her this time. Jess was furious. She said Sam had so much room and she wouldn't even notice they were there. It was like she felt entitled to whatever Sam had as if it was her own, just like she used to with Sam's clothes."

We both stood watching Benson grapple with the stick for a while. He dragged it out of the surf, then dropped it on the sand to sniff warily at a pile of seaweed. Then he noticed us looking and trotted up the beach towards us, wringing wet and happy as a clam.

"But they made up."

She shrugged and started walking again, Benson trailing behind us. "More or less. Forgiven, perhaps, but not forgotten. Sam was actually thinking of selling up and moving to Newcastle."

"Why Newcastle?"

"That's where she worked, so it would have cut her commute down dramatically. But I think the biggest reason was to get away from Jess. She'd decided it was time to get out from under her twin's shadow."

CHAPTER 22

PRIYA LOOKED BEHIND ME AS I JOINED THE CIRCLE OF CHAIRS SET up in the library that night for our book club meeting. "You didn't bring Jack? I thought he wanted to join book club?"

"I think he's working tonight. But you needn't look so disappointed—I brought something that should cheer you up."

"I'm not disappointed," she protested, but her expression brightened when I pulled the bottle of pink champagne from my bag.

She took it from me and began stripping the foil off with expert hands. "So, this is mine. What are the rest of you drinking?"

"I hope you've brought some glasses, too," Heidi said with a teasing look at Priya. "Not all of us are happy to share spit with Priya."

I'd brought some plastic ones from my picnic set and everyone soon had a glass of bubbly. We were all here—

Aunt Evie, Andrea, Heidi, Priya, Sarah, and me—except for Emily, who had tickets to the theatre and had headed down to Sydney for the weekend.

"I've always liked pink champagne," Aunt Evie said, holding her glass up to the light. "It's so festive."

"It's such a happy colour," Heidi agreed. "Like pink lemonade, except for grown-ups."

With six of us, the bottle was only enough for one glass each, but any more would probably have stretched the friendship as far as Andrea was concerned. She took book discussions seriously, and had refused to let Priya move our discussions from the library to the local hotel. She said everyone would get drunk and no one would discuss the book.

I'd given her a pretty notebook with matching pen as a belated birthday gift when I arrived, and Aunt Evie had brought a bunch of bright gerberas.

"What should we drink to?" Priya asked.

"Andrea's birthday," I said. "Happy birthday!"

There was a chorus of *Happy birthdays* around the circle.

"Was that this week?" Heidi looked dismayed. "I missed it."

"Don't worry about it," Andrea said. "It's not important."

"Did you have a nice day?"

"It was lovely. The girls at the library brought me a cake and I went out to lunch with my sister."

"Get any special gifts?" I asked slyly.

"Mum gave me a gift voucher for the spa at the Metropole. Oh, and Nick got me the new Ephram Jobbs thriller." She tossed that in like a throwaway line, but she carefully didn't meet anyone's eyes as she said it. I smiled, satisfied. Then she put her glass on the floor by her chair and cleared her throat. "If we're all ready now, perhaps we could discuss *Middlemarch*."

"I haven't read it," Priya said. "Charlie told me it was rubbish."

"I did not!"

Priya waved a lazy hand. "Something like that, anyway."

"I said it was good and I was enjoying it." I glanced defensively at Andrea, who was frowning. I felt like a kid caught doing the wrong thing at school. "How is that the same as saying it was rubbish?"

"You said it was all about married people being miserable and honestly, I've had marriage up to here at the moment." She made a dramatic gesture at chin height.

"Is your mum still hassling you?" Sarah leaned in, ready for any gossip. "Haven't you got that dinner this weekend?"

"Yeah," Heidi said. "What are you going to do about that? Have you told her yet that you don't really have a boyfriend?"

Andrea sighed, but she closed her copy of *Middlemarch* and picked up her champagne instead, bowing to the inevitable. It might be a while yet before any serious book discussion took place.

"No." Priya took a gulp of champagne then stared moodily at the bubbles in her glass. "I told her he was busy this weekend so she's put it off until the following one."

"That's good," Aunt Evie said encouragingly. "That gives you more time."

"To get a boyfriend?" I gave her an incredulous look. "In a week?"

But Aunt Evie was unfazed. "I'm sure a smart girl like Priya can come up with something."

"Yeah," Priya said. "Maybe I can move to New Zealand before then."

"Just tell her the truth," Andrea said. "You don't have a boyfriend and you don't want one either."

"That's only half true," Priya said. "I'd love to have a boyfriend, but Mum's not talking about a boyfriend. She's talking about a fiancé. And I *definitely* don't want one of those."

"She can't actually force you to marry someone if you don't want to," Heidi said. "You're a grown woman. You have rights."

"Ugh," Priya groaned. "This isn't about legalities. It's about her making my life pure hell if she doesn't get her way."

"You make her sound like a harridan," Aunt Evie said. "Amina is a lovely woman."

"I *know*," Priya said. "That's what makes it so hard. When she looks at me with those sad, disappointed eyes I can hardly bear it. She says all she wants is for me to be happy, but we don't agree on what would make me happy. She's convinced I can only be happy with a nice Hindu boy."

"Well, at least she wants a nice boy for you," Andrea said. "You could be stuck in a loveless marriage with a monster like Casaubon."

Priya gave her a blank stare. "I have no idea who you're talking about."

I grinned. "That was Andrea's very unsubtle way of trying to bring the conversation around to the book. Casaubon's one of the characters. He's a terrible husband."

"At least Dorothea didn't have a murder at *her* wedding," Sarah muttered.

"How *is* dear Molly?" Aunt Evie asked.

Molly was Sarah's sister. I'd been the photographer at her recent wedding, which had been the talk of the town after one of the guests had died at the reception. Not the greatest start to married life.

"She's good." Sarah said. "She and Marco had a fabulous time in Noosa on their honeymoon. Actually, Charlie, I've been meaning to ask if you could do a big A4-sized print for me of that photo you took of me and Molly at the wedding. I thought it would be a good Christmas present for Mum."

"Sure. No problem."

"It seems a bit mean to say it, but I think Molly's glad in a way that there's a new drama in town. Not that she would ever have wished any harm on Sam, of course. But it's nice that people have stopped talking about her wedding all the time."

"Poor Sam," Aunt Evie said. "Such a tragedy. Charlie's investigating her death."

"Aunt Evie!"

But the cat was out of the bag, and everyone wanted to know what I'd discovered. I didn't want to mention Grace.

"Honestly, guys, nothing's changed since last weekend, when we talked about this at the housewarming. I don't believe Jess is the killer and I'm sure some evidence will come to light soon that proves it."

"How can you be so sure?" Sarah asked. "Did you know that Jess got shafted by Ben Cassar, same as we did? She and Leo lost even more than we did, because they were building a bigger house."

Ben Cassar had left a trail of half-built houses and broken dreams behind him when he died. Sarah certainly hadn't shed any tears over his death.

"Yes, I'd heard. They're living with Leo's parents now."

"So who inherits Sam's house?"

"Sarah!" Heidi looked shocked. "Are you seriously suggesting Jess would kill her own sister over a house?"

Sarah shrugged. "Maybe. I tell you, after living with Mum and Dad for the last six months, I could kill anyone if it meant we could have a place of our own."

"But it was your choice to move in with them. You had that nice place on Mulberry Lane."

"Yeah, and the lease was up so we had to move out. And since Cassar had taken all our money, it made sense to live rent-free with my parents for a while so we could save up again." She shook her head. "You have no idea how gutted we were, having to start all over again. Maybe Jess was desperate. I love my parents, but living with them still isn't easy. If Jess doesn't get on with her in-laws, maybe it got too much for her."

"But it's her *sister*," Heidi said. "Her own *twin*. Zach and Noah may fight sometimes, but they're best friends. No one could be closer. The twin bond is something that other people just can't understand. It's more than having a sibling—especially if you're identical. I mean, Zach and Noah aren't, and they have a bond I've never seen in regular siblings. I can't imagine what Jess must be going through after losing that bond."

"I think twins must be like other siblings," Aunt Evie said. "A lot of them may have this wonderful bond, but there must be some that don't get along. Not everyone grows up in such a happy home as yours, Heidi."

Heidi shook her head. For once her cheerful smile was missing. "The thought of Jess going through the rest of her life without Sam makes me so sad. I just can't believe that she could be the killer. Surely the rest of you don't think she'd be capable of such an awful crime?"

She looked pleadingly around the circle.

"You know *I* don't," I said. "I think it must have been Kai." He seemed more likely than Annette or her daughter, at least.

Sarah only shrugged.

"Anything's possible," Priya said, and Andrea nodded.

Aunt Evie, who was sitting next to Heidi, patted her leg reassuringly. "I'm sure the truth will come out, dear." She smiled across at me. "Charlie will make sure it does."

Andrea drained the last of her champagne and set the glass down on the floor again. She picked up *Middlemarch*.

"Well, if that's settled, perhaps we could move on to discussing the book."

Everyone picked up their books. I stared at mine, unseeing. Aunt Evie's faith was nice and all, but what if it was misplaced?

Jess was counting on me.

CHAPTER 23

RUFUS WAS A COMPLETE BED HOG. I WOKE UP ON SATURDAY morning lying right on the edge of the bed, with him sprawled all over the middle of it.

He was also snoring. That was what had woken me.

"Hey!" I prodded him and he gave me a wounded look. "Don't look at me like that. I'm not the one stealing the bed and waking people up."

He sniffed at my hand and gave it an apologetic lick, then yawned so wide I swear I saw his intestines. Then he stood up and shook himself, raining golden hairs on my blanket. Having shed everywhere to his satisfaction, he hopped down, giving me a sort of *come on, then, what are you waiting for?* look over his shoulder.

"Not so fast, young man. Some of us need to pee."

I let him out into the backyard while I had breakfast, leaving the glass sliding door open so he could come and go as he pleased. Jack was out on his deck, also having breakfast, but I didn't say anything to him, since I was only wearing my PJs.

Much to his disgust, I left Rufus at home when I headed out. I wanted to go to Vinnies to see if I could pick up some props for my photography business cheaply—things like kids' dress-up costumes, or crocheted blankets and cushions for background texture—and the volunteers in Vinnies hadn't been as welcoming of Rufus as some of the other shops in town.

I could totally understand that—they had all kinds of china and breakable knickknacks on display. A large dog with a big, sweeping tail could wreak havoc. And then there were the racks of second-hand clothes—no one wanted to buy clothing that had dog fur all over it. Since I lived with him, I'd become resigned to the fact that dog hairs were part of my life now. No matter how often I brushed him, he only had to breathe to scatter fur all over the place. But the clientele of Vinnies probably weren't as keen on the idea.

As I opened the door to Vinnies, someone coming out almost walked straight into me.

"Grace!" I said.

She flinched when she realised it was me and gave me the same guilty look that Rufus had when he'd tried to help himself to my peanut butter toast the other morning.

"Everything all right?" I asked. She seemed in such a hurry.

She scowled at me. "Are you following me around? Because we didn't kill that lady."

"Nobody said you did." I felt a little twinge of guilt since I'd pretty much implied that in our last conversation and it had obviously rankled with her. I let the door fall shut and stepped to one side. We stood on a narrow pavement next to the council carpark and there wasn't much foot traffic here, since all the other shops in the row had their entrances on the other side of the building, on the street side. I assumed Vinnies had theirs at the back of the building because so many people pulled up in their cars right by their door to donate stuff. Anything to make it easier to receive donations was probably a good idea. "So what *did* you do? Did you steal her car from her driveway?"

"No!" She looked offended. "We never went *near* her house. We told you, we found it in the carpark at the skate ramp and took it for a ride. It had the keys in it and everything. We didn't mean any harm."

"Except for the part where you set fire to it."

"That was all Callum. I didn't want to, but he doesn't listen to me. And Josh goes along with everything Callum says."

"Uh-huh. But you took that J charm off the keyring, didn't you?" Her eyes flicked down and to the side. "Come on, tell me the truth."

"All right, that was me. But Callum was just going to chuck the keys in the bushes and it was so pretty. And it was a J. Josh never gives me anything."

I wanted to shout at her, *Then why do you want something with his initial? Get rid of him! Find somebody better.* But now was not the time for relationship counselling. And no teen girl in the throes of first love was ever going to take the advice of someone like me, anyway. I was twenty-nine, but it might as well have been fifty-nine as far as she was concerned. Both were equally ancient.

"The lady's dead now, anyway. She doesn't need it anymore." She sneaked a quick glance up at me. "Are you going to dob me in?"

"The lady may be dead, but her twin sister isn't, and she's grieving. She has a charm just like it on her own keyring, only hers is S for Sam."

"What's *her* name?"

"Jess. And those charms were very special to them both. It would mean a lot to Jess to get that back. Maybe if that charm reappears I won't need to mention to anyone where it went."

She muttered something under her breath and walked off. Hopefully she would do the right thing. I sighed and went inside.

The Saint Vincent de Paul Society operated charity shops all over Australia. Maybe other places, too, for that matter. I didn't know and had never really thought about it. Vinnies was just a fact of life. Most towns had one, staffed by volunteers who sorted the donations and manned the shop. Womanned the shop? Most of them were women, often retired, who were giving something back to their community.

When I lived in Sydney, I had always donated my unwanted clothes to Vinnies if they were still in good condition, but I'd never shopped there before. I was delighted now to discover that Sunny Bay's Vinnies had an extensive selection of secondhand books, which I hadn't noticed on my first visit, since it had been cut short by Rufus being with me. I got a little distracted and ended up with four books—none of them classics. One was a mystery and the other three were fantasy. They would keep me going for a while.

Finished with the books, I moved on to the children's clothes. I snagged a cute purple tutu with silver sparkles but there wasn't anything else of interest. From across the shop, I spied a flower crown among the hats, so I wandered over to have a look.

A bright pink cap sat on the same shelf. I picked it up, thinking of a certain cute five-year-old with her daddy's beautiful brown eyes and an unreasoning love of pink. And it had sparkles, too!

Only the sparkles were diamantes that spelled out the word *Princess*. A shiver literally ran down my spine as I stared at the familiar sight, and my breath caught in my throat. The pink cap that appeared in half the photos from my photo shoot with Sam and Jess. The pink cap that Annette had seen a blond woman wearing as she left Sam's house and drove away—after Sam was already dead.

My heart beat faster as I stared at the innocent-looking thing in my hand. Was it Jess's? Maybe she couldn't bear to keep it anymore now that Sam was dead, and she'd donated it to Vinnies. But if she was the type to get rid of sentimental items that reminded her of her sister, why would she be so cut up about the loss of the J charm from Sam's keyring—bought on the same trip, and holding all the same memories for her of happier times?

Eventually I remembered to breathe again and turned the cap over. Inside was a manufacturer's label. Over the top of the care instructions, someone had used a black sharpie to write a big, black "S".

This was Sam's cap.

Holy plot twist, Batman. Sam was dead when this cap left her house. *She* hadn't been the one to donate it to Vinnies. It must have been the killer.

Jess had her own copy of this cap. If she had been the person seen leaving Sam's house that morning, she would have worn her own. What possible reason could she have for taking her dead sister's cap? Not that I believed for a minute that the mysterious blond woman had been Jess.

The killer had needed to wear the cap to disguise the fact that, despite being blond, she wasn't Sam. I imagined her waiting inside Sam's house while Sam's body cooled under the bed, watching out the window. Perhaps she even knew that Annette was a gardener who was regularly found in her front yard watering the plants.

As soon as Annette appeared, she put on Sam's cap to hide her face and left the house, knowing that Annette would later report that Sam had been alive at that time. Was she only hoping to gain time or did she think the police wouldn't be able to pinpoint the true time of death accurately enough? No doubt she had a watertight alibi all prepared for the false time of death. Unfortunately for her, forensic knowledge was too advanced for her ruse to work for long.

Or perhaps—and what a horrible thought this was— perhaps she was actually trying to frame Jess. She'd had to wear the cap because she wasn't Jess, and now she was getting rid of the damning evidence of her deception. Personally, I would have thrown it away, but perhaps she was hoping someone else would buy it, further muddying the trail.

But if that was her plan, it had backfired spectacularly, as I now realised in a blinding instant of clarity. Jess didn't need to wear a cap to impersonate Sam. She was already a perfect replica. The fact that the killer had had to wear Sam's cap proved that Jess was innocent.

CHAPTER 24

On Tuesday morning I pulled one of my old work outfits from the closet—a black skirt and a soft pink blouse. It felt strange to put on this old corporate uniform, like a skin I'd outgrown. It didn't feel like me anymore.

But a funeral required something more than shorts and T-shirts—and it also required an ensemble free from dog hair, which was much more difficult to accomplish. I had to ward Rufus off a couple of times when he showed signs of wanting to lean lovingly against my legs. I added tiny diamond studs to my ears, thinking of the twins and their love of bling, and wore my favourite silver charm bracelet. I even added a touch of lipstick, though I didn't wear mascara. I was far too likely to cry at the funeral. Instead, I added a small packet of tissues to my handbag. Best to be prepared.

The cemetery was half an hour away, so I left early. There was no traffic like there was in Sydney to make me late, but I hated to be late for something as important as a funeral—particularly this one, when Jess had specifically asked me to come for moral support.

She'd been thrilled when I called to tell her about finding the baseball cap in Vinnies. I'd given it to the police, of course, hoping they might be able to get some fingerprints off it. Detective McGovern hadn't seemed as convinced as I was that it proved Jess's innocence.

"Someone who could kill her own sister wouldn't have a problem nicking her hat," he'd said.

"But why would she?" I was frustrated with his obtuseness. "She already had the exact same hat at home. And she didn't need a prop to help her pretend to be Sam —she looks exactly like her already! Only someone who *didn't* look like her would need to take the cap."

"Maybe she wore her own cap and this one had already been donated."

"Oh, come *on*."

"Thank you for bringing it to our attention." His tone was hard. "If you think of anything else that might help our investigation, please don't hesitate to call."

He was at the funeral, too, with his partner, a younger man whose name I didn't know. They both looked sombre in their dark suits and serious expressions. Curtis had told me before that killers often hung around the funeral services of their victims, so I wasn't surprised to see them. They would be people-watching.

"Charlie!" Jess hugged me. "Thank you for coming."

"Of course," I said. "How are you holding up?"

She gave me a tremulous smile. "I'll be glad when today is over."

She introduced me to her mum and dad, and her brother and his wife. They all wore the identical strained expressions of people trying to hold it together for each other. People who hadn't been sleeping too well. Waiting for the coroner to release the body must have been torture. How much longer would the torture of knowing Sam's killer was still free go on?

"Did I tell you that the charm from Sam's keyring turned up?" Jess said to me as we stood together outside the chapel. I'd gone off to sign the attendance book while she greeted several more people, but she had gravitated back to me. "Someone left it on Sam's front doormat. I found it when we were over there cleaning out the house."

"That's wonderful," I said. *Good job, Grace.*

"And you found her cap too. I feel like you're my good luck charm."

I smiled. "If you're feeling lucky, maybe you should check that ticket Lauren gave Sam—or have you done that already? You could be a winner."

"Yes, I must do that. I meant to do it last week, but I've mislaid the ticket and I didn't have time to search for it."

"Wasn't it inside the birthday card?" I distinctly remembered picking it up off the floor and tucking it inside Lauren's card, that awful morning when Jess and I had been sitting in Sam's house waiting for the police to arrive.

"I thought so, but it must have fallen out. It'll turn up somewhere, I expect."

The crowd swelled—Sam had been a popular person —and soon it was time to go inside for the service. Like

Detective McGovern, I found myself people-watching, too, during the ceremony—anything to distract from the eulogies, which were always the hardest part of a funeral service. It nearly broke my heart when Jess started sobbing in the middle of the first one, which was delivered by their brother. Firmly, I looked away and tried to tune out the sad words. They all said the same thing anyway: Sam was gone, cruelly taken before her time, and she would be desperately missed by the people who loved her.

I had taken a seat on the aisle towards the back of the chapel. Kai had come, defying popular opinion, which was still taking a fifty-fifty bet that he was the killer. He didn't speak to the family and they ignored him, but there was a grimness in his expression that made me feel he missed Sam very much. It was pretty brave of him to show his face, in the circumstances.

I'd seen him arrive, and noted the shiny new Jeep he drove. The poor guy couldn't catch a break. If people weren't gossiping about him being the killer, they were speculating that he was our mystery Powerball winner. His whole life was under the microscope when all he probably wanted was to curl up and mourn his girlfriend in privacy.

Or whatever Sam had been to him.

Detective McGovern and his partner stood against the back wall of the chapel. I wasn't sure how watching the backs of people's head could help the investigation, but I supposed they knew what they were doing. This wasn't their first rodeo.

Priya had come in late, too late to sit with me. I

wondered if she was here in her professional capacity. The Sunny Bay Star would be interested in the funeral. I just hoped her presence didn't upset the family.

Lauren was sitting halfway down the chapel, diagonally across from me, with a man I assumed was her husband. She was wearing sunglasses, even inside, and kept dabbing underneath them at her eyes. The gold bracelet on her wrist flashed in the light coming in from the high chapel windows. Her hair was up in a sleek chignon, held in place by an elegant pin. It was a very Audrey Hepburn-inspired look.

Sam's dad got up to deliver his own eulogy. I chewed my lip, trying not to listen to his choked-up voice talking about his little pair of angel girls. There were a few laughs in there—apparently Sam had been a bit of a handful as a kid—but soon enough his voice started to tremble, and I dived for the Order of Service, hoping to distract myself.

They had used the same photo of Sam on the cover that I had had framed for the service. That one was sitting on top of the white coffin, swamped by pink flowers. In it, she was laughing, her eyes shining, and she looked so carefree and natural. The dates of her birth and death were printed on the cover underneath the photo, and something about them tugged at my memory.

The thirtieth of November 1992. 30-11-1992. Why did that ring a bell? I didn't know anyone else with that birthday—apart from Jess, of course. I frowned at the little booklet in my hand, but nothing came to me. I looked up as I caught another flash of gold from across the aisle. That bracelet on Lauren's wrist looked a lot like my own, only hers was gold instead of silver. I'd have to have a closer look at it when we got to the wake—it must be some cheap knock-off, because my silver one had been pretty pricey, and to buy the charms in gold instead would have cost me more than I spent on my car. Still, it did look classy with the whole Audrey Hepburn thing she had going on.

Sam's dad was talking about 2000 now, memorable not only for the Y2K bug but for being the year they almost lost Sam, whose intrepid nature had led to her climbing a tree that she had no business being in. He spoke of how frightened they'd been when they'd arrived at the hospital and realised how badly injured she was.

"I'm so grateful we got more than twenty extra years with our girl," he said. "But I thought I knew then what losing her would feel like. I was wrong."

Oh, dear. I turned back to the Order of Service, but not before a tear escaped me. I wiped it away, watching the numbers dance in my blurred vision, and suddenly it came to me. Hadn't I seen these numbers on that hand-lettered sign in the newsagent's window?

Surreptitiously, I pulled out my phone and Googled. A minute later, I had the winning Powerball numbers from the first week in December.

Thirty. Eleven. Nineteen. Nine. Two. Twenty. Twenty-nine and one.

The thirtieth of November 1992. I gasped. Several people frowned at me, especially when they noticed I had my phone out. That was Sam's birthday. And the twenty? Her father had just been talking about the year 2000, clearly a significant number for Sam. I didn't know what the other two numbers represented, but I was sure they would also prove to be important in Sam's life.

These weren't just the winning numbers in the Powerball draw. They were *Sam's* numbers, the same ones that Lauren bought for her every year.

Wait. This didn't make sense. The Powerball numbers were drawn on a Thursday night. Sam had died on the Friday morning and soon after, someone in Sunny Bay became a multimillionaire—but the ticket Lauren had given her had still been in her house. I'd picked it up and put it inside the birthday card myself. So how could anyone have claimed the prize?

Surely no one would take the ticket, claim the prize, then put it back? I racked my brains, trying to remember which numbers had been on that ticket. I'd only glanced at it briefly, but I was almost certain that there'd been a thirteen, because I remembered thinking it was traditionally an unlucky number. And a seven—that was right. Seven was my favourite number, so I'd noticed it. And those were not the winning numbers.

It was odd that that ticket had gone missing now. Maybe Jess had simply misplaced it, as she thought. But I couldn't help remembering the break-in at Jess's house recently. The police had assumed the burglar had been disturbed, because nothing was missing. But what if the thief had gotten exactly what they'd come for, and the ticket was the goal?

I put my phone away, still thinking furiously. I had the infuriating feeling that I was close to the answer, but things weren't quite clicking into place yet. Why would someone steal a ticket that wasn't the winning one?

Perhaps I was creating a conspiracy where none existed. Maybe Lauren had bought a few tickets at once and accidentally put the wrong one inside Sam's card. That would mean Lauren must be our mysterious winner. I narrowed my eyes, examining that gold bracelet as best I could from this distance. Maybe it was real, and she was wearing a fortune around her wrist.

The explanation could be as simple as that. But then another one occurred to me, and I stared at the back of Lauren's sleek head in shock.

CHAPTER 25

THE WAKE WAS BEING HELD AT THE LIGHTHOUSE CAFÉ, WHICH was almost all the way back home again. It stood on a cliff at the edge of Waterloo Bay. It was still a working lighthouse, but its workings had been automated many years ago. The caretaker's cottage had been turned into a museum with a café attached, and there was a glorious view back down the coast towards Sydney from the large open dining space of the café.

A huge anchor was set into the lawn in front of the lighthouse, and I recognised it as the place where Sam and Lauren had posed for the photo that Sam had kept in her dining room, their long teenage limbs browned by the sun, their faces aglow with health and happiness. I stopped and ran a hand over the warm metal of the anchor, remembering their cheeky little bikinis. Had they been taken to the café after a long day at the beach, perhaps for an ice-cold drink to cool off? Who had taken the photo? Someone's parents, or had it been Jess, already relegated to the outskirts of their relationship? There had been an almost gloating air to Lauren's expression, now I thought about it.

"Are you okay?" Priya asked, coming up the path from the car park.

"Fine. Or as fine as you can be at a funeral." I couldn't tell her what was going through my head. It was all so preposterous.

"It was a lovely service, wasn't it?"

"Mm-hmm." No need to mention either that I'd spent a lot of it actively ignoring the proceedings in favour of my own wild theories. "Are you here on official duties?"

"No. Well, only partially. I was friends with Jeremy, the brother, before he got married and moved away, so I thought I'd come along and show some support. And the Star will be happy to get a piece about the funeral." I frowned at her. "I'm not going to say much, nothing too intrusive or personal. Just the facts." She smiled at a couple who passed us heading towards the café entrance. "Are you coming?"

"In a minute." I was waiting to see if I could catch Lauren as she arrived and ask her the question that was scalding my tongue with its urgency. Surely I must be wrong. Detective McGovern would tell me I was jumping to conclusions again.

I should tell him my suspicions. But what if I was wrong? It was a terrible accusation to make about anyone. He arrived just then, stalking up the path with his partner at his side. He nodded at me but didn't say anything.

When Lauren and her husband did finally arrive, they were in the centre of a large group of friends who all swirled up the path together and into the café. Disgruntled, I followed them.

Soft music was playing from the café speakers. It might have been Vivaldi. The space had been rearranged for Sam's wake. Cakes, scones, and delicate sandwiches cut into triangles were set out on tables that had been pushed back against the wall of the building. A tea and coffee-making station was set up on another table. Some chairs had been set out around the perimeter of the space, but most people stood and moved around, chatting to each other. I took a sandwich from a tray and munched without really tasting it, watching Lauren and trying to look as though I wasn't.

Finally I had my chance. She left her group and headed up the narrow steps that led to the toilets, which were tucked away at the side of the lighthouse. I followed and waited outside the door until she came out again.

"Oh," she said, putting her hand to her chest. Her bracelet caught my eye. Up close, I could tell it was the real deal. "You startled me."

I didn't move aside, which meant she was trapped in the narrow hallway, unable to reach the stairs. Her smile dimmed, replaced by confusion.

"Congratulations," I said.

"On what?"

"Winning the lottery." I watched her face carefully.

"I don't know what you mean," she said, but there was a flash of surprise in her eyes, quickly hidden.

Disappointment and rage warred within me. I had no doubt now, and I was *mad*. How *could* she? I'd have given anything to be wrong.

"That's a beautiful bracelet. I remember checking out that seashell charm when I was buying charms for this one." I held up my wrist to show her. "That little diamond makes it expensive, doesn't it? And solid gold, too. Was it eight hundred and fifty or nine hundred and fifty? I can't remember now. I know I couldn't afford even one gold charm, much less a whole bracelet full of them."

She stared at me for a long moment. "It's a birthday present."

"Someone must really like you. Who's it from?"

"My husband, not that it's any of your business."

"Oh?" I pretended to examine my nails. "That would be the husband who couldn't afford any more IVF treatments?" She'd forgotten she'd told me about that, hadn't she? But I had a good memory. "And now he's throwing around jewellery worth thousands of dollars? That husband?"

She drew in a sharp breath, probably preparing to spin me another line, but I cut her off.

"Was it worth killing your best friend for a bracelet?"

"Are you out of your *mind*?" But her face had gone stark white.

The sweet strains of classical music floated up the stairs. So genteel. So delicate. It made this confrontation in a dark and rather dingy corridor feel surreal. I could hear the clink of tea cups, too, and the soft murmur of voices, like the sighing of waves on the sand.

"That day when you stopped on the way home from your conference to chat to me—that wasn't the first time you'd snuck out of the conference, was it? You came home early Friday morning as soon as you realised Sam had won the Powerball. You probably parked in your own driveway and ran straight down the street to Sam's, determined to get that ticket back. Back in the Hunter Valley, everyone was still in bed or having their breakfast. I'm guessing the official conference program didn't even start until nine o'clock. No one missed you."

"Get out of my way," she said through gritted teeth, but I refused to budge.

"You put your hair up afterwards, didn't you? Shoved it up out of the way under Sam's favourite cap, so that you'd look more like her. You probably knew that Annette was half-blind anyway—you live in the same street. And then you dumped it in the donation bin at Vinnies to get rid of it. That was a mistake, by the way. You should have chucked it in the rubbish somewhere."

"I don't have to listen to this." She tried to push past me, but I stood firm.

"Just like you dumped her car. Pretty clever leaving it next to the skate park with the keys in it. That just about guaranteed someone would steal it. What was that about, by the way?" I kept my voice to an easy, conversational tone, though it was an effort. I genuinely wanted to know, and I hoped she might tell me once she realised the game was up. "Were you just trying to confuse the time of death?" My anger crept into my voice, despite my best efforts. "After you shoved your supposed best friend under the bed like a cast-off shoe?"

She stared at me, shaking. "It wasn't like that!" she burst out, then she flew at me, clawing at me like an animal desperate to escape a trap.

I yelped as she shoved at me. I'd been braced, half-expecting something like this, so she didn't manage to tip me down the stairs behind me, but it was a close thing.

"Hey," a deep voice said behind me. "What are you doing?"

Kai bounded up the last few steps and shoved Lauren off me. She lashed out at him and he caught at her arm. The golden bracelet snapped and flew across the hallway, where it hit the toilet door and dropped to the floor.

"Let *go* of me," she demanded.

"What's going on here?" he asked, holding her against the wall easily with one muscled arm.

"She killed Sam," I said.

It was out of my mouth before I considered who I was talking to. He let out a roar of animal rage and slammed her against the door so that it rattled. The noise of conversation downstairs abruptly cut off, though the gentle music continued to play as footsteps belted up the stairs.

"Detective McGovern," I said as Lauren screamed and sobbed. "I'm glad to see you."

He took stock of the situation immediately and separated Kai from Lauren, but she continued to wail.

"I didn't mean it," she cried in between sobs. "You have to believe me. It was an accident. She fell."

"Why did you hide the body, then?" I demanded.

"What on earth is going on?" Detective McGovern asked.

She covered her face and moaned. "I panicked. I didn't know what to do. I didn't mean it!" Her voice rose again. "I didn't mean it!"

I almost felt sorry for her. Almost.

"But you didn't report it, did you? Because you wanted that ticket. You gave it to Sam for her birthday, but you wanted it back." I leaned in, desperate to get to the truth before Detective McGovern came over all official and ruined it.

"What ticket?" he asked. "What are you talking about?"

Kai shushed him. His face was grim but his eyes were clear again. He wanted to know just as much as I did, if not more.

"The winning lottery ticket," I said, never taking my eyes from her face. We were all crowded into the narrow hallway together, oddly intimate. Kai was breathing in deep, ragged breaths. Even I was shaking at the intensity of the moment. "She always gave a ticket to Sam for her birthday. Always used the same numbers. So she knew, as soon as she found out what the winning numbers were, that Sam had won." I dragged Lauren's hands away from her face and pinned her with a hard stare. "You went there to take that ticket back, didn't you?"

"No, I didn't. I swear." She stared at me, her eyes swimming with tears. "I was happy for her. For us. We had a deal, you see. We always said that if one of us won big, we'd split the prize fifty-fifty. I went there to celebrate."

"And what happened?"

"She went back on the deal. She said she'd give me fifty grand." Lauren was shaking her head from side to side now like an animal in pain. "Fifty grand! When she had seven million. It wasn't *fair*. We fought. There was a struggle. In her ... in her living room. I pushed her and she fell. She hit her head on the corner of the coffee table." Her eyes were wild. "I didn't mean it. I didn't mean to hurt her. But I was angry and she fell and I could tell straight away that she was dead."

Kai made a sound, almost a whimper. It sounded strange and wrong coming from the mouth of a powerful, dangerous-looking guy like him.

"So instead of calling for help, you cleaned up the blood, hid the body, and waltzed out of there with the winning ticket. What was the other ticket, by the way? The one that was in the birthday card?"

"Just one I had in my wallet. I left it there to replace the one I took. I thought Jess might remember there was supposed to be one there and get suspicious if there wasn't. But then I thought better of it when she told you about our system. I didn't want anyone to realise it was the wrong ticket. So I took it back."

"You stole it? You were the one who broke into Jess's in-laws' house?"

She looked down at the floor and her voice was a whisper. "Yes."

I sagged back against the wall and exchanged a look with Detective McGovern. He looked almost shell shocked. I couldn't even look at Kai. He had turned his face away. What a nightmare this was for him—but at least that other nightmare was over, the one where he was suspected of killing Sam himself.

Detective McGovern cleared his throat. "Right. I think we'd better take this conversation down to the station."

CHAPTER 26

Hours later, I left the police station. I had seven missed calls on my phone. Just about everyone I knew had called me. Word had spread fast. Priya had called twice, threatening to disembowel me if I didn't ring her the *minute* I was home.

I let myself in the front door and dropped my keys and handbag on the dining table. Rufus was barking at the back door, totally convinced that he would never eat again. I opened the door and he bounded in, doing his best to convince me that he hadn't eaten in at least three years.

"In a minute, boy." I flopped down on the couch and pulled off my shoes. They weren't my highest pair of heels by any means, but I'd been in them for *hours*, and it was a long time since I'd worn heels at all. My toes shrieked in sweet relief as I wriggled them. "I'm sorry. I know it's past your dinner time. I wasn't expecting to be gone this long."

It was past my dinner time, too, but I wasn't sure I had the energy to cook. It was shaping up to be a peanut butter toast kind of night. The police had been kind but very thorough, and I was absolutely wrung out from answering their questions. I let my head fall back against the couch cushions with a thud. Maybe I should sleep down here tonight. Climbing the stairs to my bedroom felt as strenuous as attempting Mount Everest.

Rufus, of course, didn't care how draining my day had been. A dog could very well fade away into mere skin and bone if due precautions weren't taken, and he was prepared to shove his wet nose into my face as many times as necessary to ensure I levered myself off the couch and fed him.

I was doing just that when the doorbell rang.

"Who can that be?" I groaned as I put his bowl on the floor.

It might have been Genghis Khan and the entire Mongol horde as far as Rufus was concerned. He was too busy scarfing his food down to care. I dreaded the thought of talking to a single other person tonight, but I dragged myself to the door and opened it.

Priya barged in, trailing the tantalising scent of pizza from the box she carried. "I figured you'd be beat after spending all afternoon at the police station, so I brought food."

"You're an angel," I said. "Tell your mother not to worry about the nice Hindu boy; I'm marrying you myself."

She grinned, a flash of white teeth against brown skin, and clattered around in the kitchen cupboards until she found two plates, which she brought to the table. I collapsed into a chair and started on the pizza while she opened the fridge and stood frowning for a moment.

"Wait right here," she said.

And then she walked out the front door.

The pizza was delicious—covered with olives and sun-dried tomatoes, and dripping cheese. I was too tired to be curious about what she was up to, but I didn't have to wait long to find out. In a moment she was back, with Jack trailing behind her, and he carried two bottles of champagne.

Surprisingly, Sherlock snuck in on his heels. The cat stalked into the kitchen, saw Rufus head-down in his bowl, and did an abrupt about-face. He ensconced himself on the back of one of my couches instead and gave me a flat stare, daring me to suggest he was afraid of an insignificant beast like Rufus.

"Sherlock, what are you doing?" Jack asked. He looked at me. "I'm sorry, he doesn't usually leave the house. I'll take him home before he gets hair all over your furniture."

"Don't worry about it," I said. "He could shed every hair on his body and it still wouldn't compare to Rufus's efforts."

Jack still looked concerned. "Will Rufus mind a cat in his territory?"

I gestured at the dog, who was ignoring all of us while in single-minded pursuit of the last few pieces of kibble in his bowl. "Does he look like he minds?"

Jack relaxed and held up one of the bottles of champagne like Exhibit A at a science fair. "I had a couple of bottles of champers left from the housewarming. Priya seemed to think you might need a drink."

I smiled gratefully at him. "Glasses are in that cupboard above the fridge. Want some pizza?"

"I just ate," he said, but he still took a slice after he'd poured three glasses.

"This is wonderful," I said as the food began to revive me. "But now I don't know which one of you to marry."

Jack looked startled but Priya laughed. "Me, of course. I'm the mastermind behind all this."

I grabbed another slice. "You're right. As long as you're not a criminal mastermind, we're sweet."

She cocked her head to one side. "Speaking of criminals ..."

"Ah. I knew there would be a payment for this wonderful meal. You want the goss."

"She knows me so well," Priya said to Jack.

"The whole town is buzzing with rumours," Jack said. "If even I heard them at the hospital, it's got to be big. What on earth happened at that funeral?"

"First tell me what happened at the wake after I left," I said to Priya.

She shrugged and pulled a great string of cheese off the end of her pizza slice. "Not much. McGovern and his partner marched the three of you off to the station, and everyone saw what a mess Lauren was. A couple of people heard some of what happened upstairs and suddenly everyone knew that Lauren was under arrest. The family pretty much left en masse after that."

"I think most of them came to the police station," I

said. "I saw Jess and her parents there at one stage, but Detective McGovern wouldn't let me talk to them."

"Short of the body sitting up in the coffin, I don't think the wake could have been any more sensational. What happened up there? We could all hear Lauren screaming and someone else shouting. It sounded like another murder."

I filled them in on the details. There didn't seem much point in keeping it confidential. I was sure the police had already told the family what had happened and what we'd learned—and it wasn't as though anyone in Sunny Bay would be called on to serve as a juror at Lauren's trial.

Jack's eyes grew wider and wider as I spoke. Priya just kept refilling the champagne.

"But how did she expect to keep the money a secret?" Priya asked. "Everyone's been trying to figure out who won. The minute she started spending, the secret would have been out."

We were well into the second bottle by then and I was feeling very mellow. "I suppose it wouldn't have mattered eventually. As long as no one figured out that the winner should have been Sam, she was fine. If she could keep it secret for even a few months, no one would ever have put it together."

"Just as well we have you," Priya said. We had moved into the lounge room by this stage, and she was slumped on the couch opposite me, leaning against Jack. Sherlock had made himself comfortable in her lap. "She's the best detective the police force never had," she told Jack solemnly. "At this point, they ought to be paying her."

"Very impressive work," he agreed. "You should give up photography and become a great detective instead."

"No, thanks." I curled my feet up under me on the couch. "Photography is a lot more fun than dead bodies."

Priya pointed at me. "I need to do a feature on you."

"No way. Let Detective McGovern have the credit. The only thing I want to be known for is taking beautiful photos and having the most successful photography business on the coast."

Priya pouted. "But think what it could do for my career."

"Never mind your career. What about our marriage? I'll divorce you if you nag me about it."

"Poor Priya," Jack said, grinning. "always with the marital troubles." He slung a friendly arm around her shoulders.

She threw her arm across her eyes in a theatrical gesture and groaned. "Don't remind me."

"Any change in that area?" I asked. "Have you spoken to your mother?"

"Absolutely not." She removed her arm to give me a withering look. "Do I look like an idiot?"

"Do you really want me to answer that?"

"Haha."

"Priya, it's Tuesday night. In four more nights, you'll be at dinner with your parents and you'll have to produce a boyfriend. How exactly are you going to work this piece of magic?"

She wriggled around so she could peer rather blearily

up into Jack's face. "What are you doing on Saturday night?"

I sat up straight. "Oh, no. Priya, you can't."

"Why not?" She sat up straighter herself, grinning as she warmed to the idea. "You don't have a girlfriend, do you?" she asked him.

"Nooo?" Maybe it was the champagne, but it took him a minute to catch on. "Oh. You want me to ... pretend to be your boyfriend?"

"In a nutshell," she said.

"But what about after that?" I asked. "He's a nurse, and your mum's a doctor. What if he sees her at the hospital?"

"Relax. She's a GP. She doesn't go to the hospital any more than you or I." She patted him on the knee. "It will be fine. Just one dinner, and then I'll tell her you're working any time she asks after that. You're a shift worker, so that checks out." She treated him to her brightest smile. "What do you say?"

He grinned back at her. "Sure. I'm game."

I picked up the nearest cushion and buried my face in it. "I just know this is going to end badly."

"Oh, shush, Cassandra. Everything will be fine."

"Those sound like famous last words to me. But what do I know? I'm just a normal person—"

"Who goes around solving crimes," Priya said.

"So really you're like a crime-fighting superhero," Jack agreed. "*You* should have a cat called Sherlock, not me."

"And you can be her Mr Watson," Priya crowed.

"I thought I was *your* Mr Watson." There was something in his voice that brought the colour to Priya's cheeks.

I shook my head and held out my glass. "I'm going to need more champagne for this. A *lot* more champagne."

THE END

KEEP up to date with new releases, special deals and other book news by signing up for my newsletter at www.emeraldfinn.com.

Reviews and word of mouth are vital for any author's success. If you enjoyed *Blondes, Bikinis and Betrayal,* please take a moment to leave a short review where you bought it. Just a few words sharing your thoughts on the book would be extremely helpful in spreading the word to other readers (and this author would be immensely grateful!).

Come and chat with me and other cozy mystery lovers in the friendly Facebook group A Pocketful of Cozies. We'd love to have you!

ACKNOWLEDGEMENTS

Thanks to my husband Mal and my daughter Jen for beta reading, and to my dear friend Jen Rasmussen for her excellent and insightful editing.

There must be something magic about the name "Jen"—both these Jens are awesome people as well as mystery mavens. Their comments and suggestions helped me make this a better book.

As for Mal—I don't need to win the Powerball (although I wouldn't say no!). I won life's lottery already when I married him.

About the Author

Emerald Finn loves books, tea, and chocolate, not necessarily in that order. Oh, and dogs. And solving mysteries with the aid of her trusty golden retriever. No, wait. That last bit might be made up.

In fact, Emerald herself is made up, though it's absolutely true that she loves books, tea, chocolate, and dogs. Emerald Finn is the pen name of Marina Finlayson, who writes books full of magic and adventure under her real name. She shares her Sydney home with three kids, a large collection of dragon statues, and the world's most understanding husband.

Made in the USA
Monee, IL
17 June 2022